Nine Deadly Sins
An Eye for an 'I'

Steve Tanham

Their meetings are necessarily brief... seldom no more than a coffee, a momentary pause between the demands of life and work... but for John and Alexandra time matters less than the connection they share...

Why Nine Deadly Sins, when the world speaks of only seven? When John and Alexandra meet for coffee, a challenge is issued that will take them on a strange journey into the depths of the human psyche.

These coffee-break encounters bring to life the mysteries of the spiritual enneagram as explored by the Silent Eye, a modern Mystery school.

Nine Deadly Sins was originally published in serial form on the website of The Silent Eye, an international School of Consciousness, founded by Steve Tanham, offering a correspondence course and online teaching seeking to bring awareness of the magic inherent in everyday life.

thesilenteye.co.uk

NINE DEADLY SINS

An Eye for an 'I'

Steve Tanham

Nine Deadly Sins

Part One

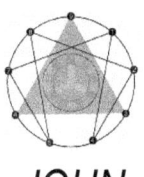

JOHN

One

"I read the brochure for the workshop," she said, trying to look only partly interested. It's a long-practiced routine between us, this mutual act of mind-fishing.

"Ah, good," I replied.

She sipped her coffee, waiting for my silence to break . . . Nothing . . .

" . . . And I don't understand the significance of that funny circle thingy," she said, irritated that her half hour in the coffee shop was being eaten up by my exasperating ways.

"The ennea-thingy?" I asked, all innocence.

"Yes, dammit, the ennea-thingy!" she whooshed–yes whooshed.

"Would you like me to explain it?" I asked her; then added, looking slyly at my watch, "Well, as much of it as we can fit into the remaining fifteen minutes?"

"Yes . . ." The tone was flat, for fear of losing more time. "I'd like that."

"From one very interesting perspective, it's all about the nine deadly sins," I said, watching to see if she spotted the humour. She didn't . . .

Instead, she asked, reasonably, "Aren't there supposed to be seven?"

"There were originally eight." I sipped my own latté, in no hurry at all. I wasn't trying to be difficult, but with Alexandra, you have to be slow and deliberate or she will race off at a tangent. I wanted her to digest what I was saying, coming back for more rather than hurrying it. I continued, "The original list was: gluttony, lust, avarice, sadness, anger, acidia, vainglory, and pride." I could see her filing them away, her lips moving in silent repetition as her well-ordered mind did its recording.

The wind and rain pounded the seafront cafe's windows. She glanced up at the streaming glass, frowning at the thought of her onward journey in the rain. She shook her head to clear away the unwelcome distraction.

"But you just said nine?"

"I did. The Desert Fathers, who invented them to protect the core of the teachings in the centuries after Christ, are said to have left out or concealed the hidden one."

"A hidden sin?" she said, looking at me with snaky eyes. "This is not going to be quick, is it?"

"No," I replied, "But it will be fun . . ."

"Fun as in a deadly sin?" her grin was wicked. She was returning to form.

"Fun as in the deadly sin as signpost." I replied, knowing that she would not be able to resist the hint of adventure.

"Signpost?"

"Signpost . . ."

She drew a breath before saying, "So there were originally eight, but they missed one, so it's really nine, but the world only recognises seven of them anyway–and all this is about that geometrical ennea-thingy?"

"Precisely!" I said, nodding my encouragement and driving her nuts.

"Where does the first signpost point?" She grasped at it, trying for something concrete she could file away as exhibit A. She was a barrister, after all. I watched her let the air escape from her lungs in a long sigh, calming herself. We had known each other for a long time. I tried to deliver what she needed from my odd and eclectic knowledge, but it wasn't always what she wanted.

I held up a vertical finger. "Good question." I said. "The answer depends on whether we start at midnight or not."

"Midnight?"

I took off my watch. I had to start being more helpful and less infuriating or I would end up wearing her coffee cup. I placed the watch by her saucer, with the twelve position facing her. "What's at the top of the watch?" I asked.

"Top . . . Oh I see, twelve!" she said, then added quickly, grasping the point, "As in how we look at it on our wrist–as in not one . . ."

"Just so. We see it every day, but the watch hand begins with the highest number, rather than the lowest–which in this case would be a one."

"And the ennea-thingy?" she asked, beginning to get my point.

"Begins with its highest number, too . . ."

"As in nine!" she chortled, triumphantly. She grabbed a spare serviette, whipped her pen out of her suit pocket, drew a quick circle and stabbed the pen at the top, turning the wound into a figure nine.

"Just so," I nodded my approval.

She smiled. "So, where does the nine signpost point?"

I shook my head. "It would spoil all the fun," I said unreasonably.

"Spoil my fun, you mean!" There was a slight flaring of the nostrils. Under other circumstances I would have been in trouble.

"No," I protested. "Missing your train . . ." I pointed at my watch, still lying on the table near her.

"Sod it," she grumbled, realising she would have to go or miss her train to London.

"Same time next week?" I offered, as olive branch.

"You're buying the coffee," she winked at me, pleased that her mock anger had achieved the desired result. "A week is . . ."

I stole the pause. "Too long, but it will be worth it . . ." I blew Alexandra a kiss and fastened the watch back on my wrist, smiling as she flew through the door, and out into the gale, bags in hand.

It would, indeed, be worth it . . .

Two

She must have been sitting there a while when I arrived for our regular Monday morning get-together. Her coffee was half finished. The one she had bought for me was full, but no longer hot.

"Keen, or am I late?" I asked, with what I hoped she'd see was a warm smile. She was used to the power of words, to the polarity of debate. She was not about to let the early advantage slip away so easily. So she said nothing . . . the pale brown eyes looked at me calmly.

"Aha," I said, not wanting to waste her precious half hour before the train, and conscious that, when working with anyone as competent as Alexandra, it's important to know when to bend. "Okay . . ." I sat down, took a sip from my coffee cup and took my watch off, lying it in front of her. "I thought I was buying?" I said.

In reply, she took out the serviette on which she had done the hasty drawing last week.

The circle with the stabbed '9' had faded a little in the pocket of the busy suit, but was quite recognisable. Alexandra rested the point of her pen on the numeral and fixed me with a cat-like stare.

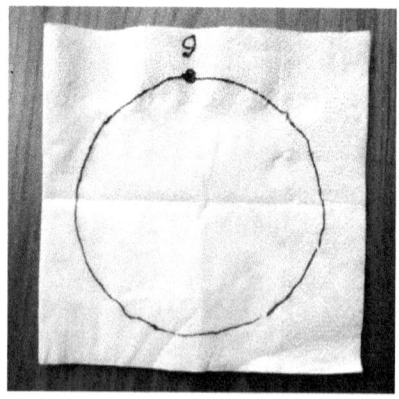

"Signpost."

"Signpost?"

"Stop playing bloody games, you know what I want to know."

I was ready for the outburst. I leaned forward and whispered, "We can't start with the '9' signpost."

"You promised!"

"I did and I will, but we have to build back up to the nine or it won't have as much power as it deserves . . ." Now I wasn't playing, and she sensed the shift.

"Why are we whispering?" she asked.

"Because the nine and its meaning are part of the secret."

"The wicked secret? The missing one of the nine that was eight that thinks it's seven?"

"Yes, that one . . ."

She drank some coffee and looked less bullet-proof. "What can we start with, then?'

"Well, apart from the nine, they are all equally good start points."

Alexandra sipped some thoughtful coffee, composing her next question. But I pre-empted her:

"What's your favourite sin?"

"We're not getting personal, I hope?"

"Not in the least, 'favourite' in terms of, perhaps, a fascination?"

When it came, I was proud of her answer. As a barrister, I wouldn't have expected anything else.

"Lying . . ." she said, softly; suddenly looking very serious. "People lie all the time."

"Just to others?" I coaxed.

"No," she smiled, getting my drift. "To themselves, too . . . "

"And which does the most damage?"

I watched the importance of the realisation flicker across her face. "To themselves . . . " It was one of those moments that tell you that you are most certainly not wasting your time.

"Yes, so draw the nine points on your circle and I'll show you where lying lives."

Her brow furrowed, "Nine points, just anywhere?"

"Now come on; why would 'just anywhere' not be a good idea?"

"No symmetry?" she replied. "And there's something deep in the symmetry?"

"Quite . . ."

"But I'm not good at dividing the circumference of a circle into nine lengths of arc."

I was proud of her verbal precision. "You don't have to," I said. "All you have to do is divide it into three and add in some twos"

"Into three is easier?" she was looking troubled.

"It is if you create a triangle, point up, with equal sides."

She leapt on it. The pen flashed and before us appeared an extension of the wounded nine which had spawned two children, one lower left; the other lower right.

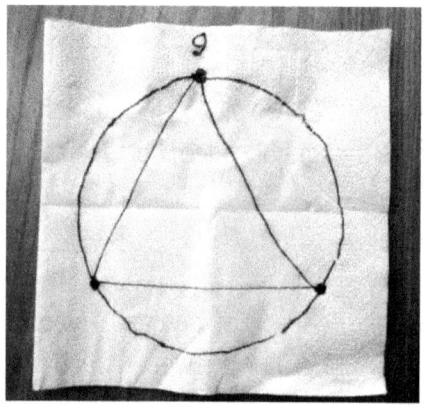

"Very good." I said.

"I could do it better on the computer?"

"And we will–but for now, the pen is mightier . . ."

"More personal?"

I nodded and took some more coffee. "And that's important at this stage, if we are not to see it as 'just another symbol'."

"What is it, really, the ennea-thingy" she asked. Her eyes were giving me that soft look, again–the one that makes me want to tell it all, to satisfy that deep hunger, but I had to make each meeting count, they had said that . . .

"What is it really? I'll tell you at the end."

"The end of all these talks?" There was a sadness in her tone.

"No, the end of today's coffee . . ."

Her face lit up, again. She leaned forward and said, "The home of 'lying' - you were going to tell me where it lived . . ."

"On the three."

"Which is?"

"Count clockwise from nine and remember you are missing three sets of two." She took a while to think about that, but her fierce intellect worked on it and, with confidence, she filled in the missing 'one' and 'two' as blue blobs, then labelled the '3'.

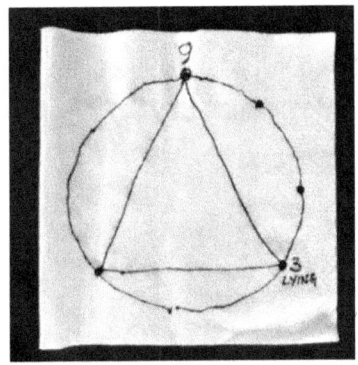

"There!" She said triumphantly, holding up the serviette, now with the word "Lying" written in lawyers' block capitals next to the 'three'.

"Keep on like this and you'll have the whole schema in no time," I said, draining the last of my coffee. "Mind you, that's just the start, without emotions nothing will happen . . ."

She had seen me tap my watch. She folded the napkin diagram back into her pocket. I was proud of the reverence with which she did so. Then, she stood, slipped into her raincoat, and took hold of the handles of the expensive black leather bags, preparing to return to her weekday world; a city-centric world I had retired from, not long ago, to help people understand the ennea-thingy and other, related topics.

"It's a signpost, don't forget . . ." I said.

Her eyes were like small fires in their intensity.

"I know, but now that I have a start point, what does it point to?"

There was only time for the simplest of responses.

"To the place where 'lying' came from, of course; like a journey taken in reverse . . ."

I watched her wrestle to remember every nuance of my answer. She wasn't trying to figure it out - not yet - there would be time for that on the train to London, it was the exactness of the memory that she sought, now.

"And the truth of the whole of the ennea-thingy?" She hadn't forgotten. It was what made her such a delight to work with.

"The *truth* of it is that the ennea-thingy is really a Truth Machine."

I waved and watched her carry it with her as she swept out into the wet March morning.

Through the briefly open door, I could see that the sun was trying its best to warm the dark waves of Morecambe Bay.

Three

Alexandra had texted me to say that she was already at the coffee shop, if I was around . . . the message also said, "Anything that purports to be a Truth Machine is worthy of a little prep."

Despite this, when I arrived it was just after 08:30, the car park machine having eaten my first lot of change without giving me back a ticket. It was one of life's little happenings; the sort that could trigger useless anger - something I very much wanted us to talk about, given the stressful life that I knew Alexandra led.

I arrived to find her sitting at our usual table. Spread out before her was a new serviette, a blank CD, a small ruler and a pen. She had reconstructed our previous drawing with more accuracy than the totally freehand approach allowed, yet was still being true to our principle of the hand's touch being important.

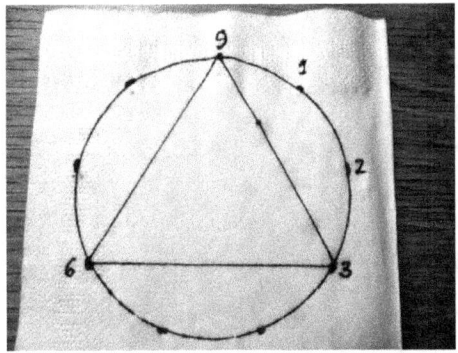

She fixed me with an amused stare. "Better?" she asked me, with a glint in her eye.

"That's really quite professional looking . . ."

She passed me my coffee. I sipped it while she filled in the numbers '1' and '2'; dividing the arc from '9' to '3' into three equal segments.

"Homework finished!" she said, truthfully. "Now why doesn't 'lying' feature in the list of sins you gave me?"

It was a very acute observation, and no less than I expected. "So is 'lying' the only one missing?" I chuckled.

"I looked up a modern list," she said with a smile, pleased to be one step ahead of me. "It was given as: wrath, greed, sloth, pride, lust, envy and gluttony - no lying!"

"Not even in its more generic description - 'deceit'?" I asked, innocently.

I watched her mentally scanning the list. "Nope," she said, with a reassured grin. "No deceit in there!"

"Well that's funny," I added. "Because the one it points backwards to, in the signpost sense, isn't in the list either . . ."

I watched her sinking. But then she grabbed the pen, again, and drew an arrow with a 'B' attached to it on the line from '3' to '6'. "It's a signpost, right?" she said. "So, it goes backward, hence my 'B' . . . She carried on with the strategy, adding another signpost between '6' and '9'. "So, presumably, it carries on pointing backwards–"

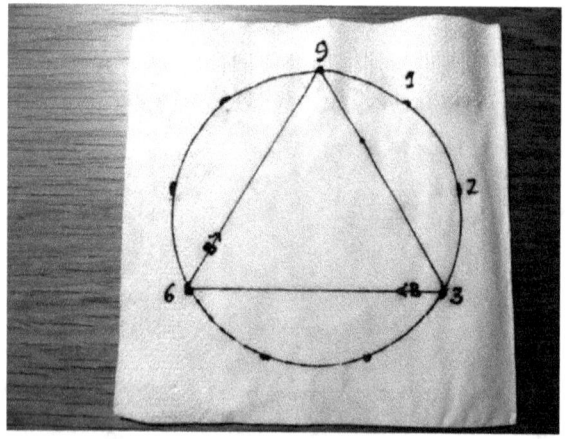

"But then there's the '9', she said, accusingly. "About which you have refused to tell me anything!"

"The wounded '9'?" I added, alluding to her initial stabbing of that point on the circle's crown - an action that would have interesting consequences about how we explored the inner and very sacred message of the symbol . . .

"The wounded '9' . . . about which I know very little, then . . ." I watched her absorb this new information, before she continued with, "But the '6' you owe me . . ."

"I do, indeed."

"So, tell me, when the '3' signpost points back at '6' as its origin, what is it pointing at?"

"It's pointing at that which produced it - it's pointing at Fear."

"The nature of point '6' is fear?" she asked, leaning forward. "Lying–deceit, then, is produced by fear?"

I sipped some more coffee before answering her hawk-like swoop on my answer.

"Yes . . ."

"Just 'yes'?"

"No, much more . . ."

This time, and with immaculate restraint, she waited. Looking at my watch, I calculated how much it would be fair to say. Very little, I decided, but it would be good.

"Deceit is running away from Fear," I said, tapping my watch. "And Fear is running away from something much more potent . . ."

"More potent than fear?" she asked in a whisper.

"Much more - and it's one of the seven, and not hidden at all . . . unlike its two children . . ."

She looked at my watch and let her breath out in a subvocal hiss.

"Quite . . ." I said finishing my coffee. I stood up, picked up the watch, blew her a kiss and left. I had no reason to leave before she did, it just felt appropriate . . .

I knew that, behind me in the coffee shop, the silence would be deafening.

Four

"It's the fear thing, isn't it?" Alexandra had me pinned into the corner of the coffee shop as though she was about to administer the final legal blow in a key case. I was even worried that my glass of water, bought to wash down the final sip of coffee, Italian style, would get spilled.

"Whenever you really think about fear, you realise that it's at the heart of so many things that people–that I–do!" She continued. I watched her become conscious, not just of what she was saying, but of how defensively she was saying it.

Seeing this happen to her, sharing the act of deeper consciousness, was a catalyst. It always was with people taking this path for the first time. Still saying nothing, I looked on, a passive and friendly observer, letting her have the space to come to terms with how central 'fear' was to her life; and to everyone else's.

Then I saw the glow of self-knowing dawn in her eyes. I watched her relax as, mentally and emotionally, she stepped back from identifying with what was happening to being the watcher of someone to whom it was happening.

"So who the bloody hell am I, then?" she blurted out, laughing, as though I had verbalised my thoughts. "If I can watch myself getting tied up in knots about the revelation of the power that fear has over me?"

It was the question of the month. It was probably one of the questions of her lifetime, though I was certainly not going to say that. I was not driving this encounter - she was.

I was simply the safe space in which it could happen ...

Her finger was pressed firmly on the '6' corner of the core triangle at the heart of the enneagram. It had been so for several minutes, while the emotion she was showing as enthusiasm raged through her. The crushed white paper was wearing thin ...

"Hold it," I said softly.

"I've just started–" she blurted out.

"No, hold it - how you feel at this instant - hold on to it and explore it!"

Again, I watched the initial moments of self-knowing wash over her.

"Something extraordinary happened, didn't it?" She sipped furiously at her tea. She must have been hungry, before I arrived, as the remains of an impromptu breakfast involving ice cream lay in front of her. "Just then . . back then."

I reached over and gently touched the white fingers that were clutching the cool cup. Professional people, who were used to the rigours of constant 'have tos' often react in this way. The touch broke the spell of her tension and she laughed.

"It's not just the initial glimpse of a deeper level of ourselves," I explained. "It's often the shock that something so fundamental to our very lives has gone unobserved for most of that time."

She freed one hand, then placed it over my calming fingers and squeezed. Her breathing returned to normal and she finished her tea, looking at me, intensely.

"So the whole of the '6' corner is about fear?"

"And its variants . . . ."

"Variants?"

"Yes, " I said, not wanting to cover too much, too soon. She, on the other hand, was very fond of darting around.

"Variants that people know under different guises."

I sat a moment, drinking some of my coffee, thoughtfully, to slow down the pace; watching her relax a little more as she waited, patiently.

"We're jumping around a bit," I said, eventually. "But, for example, one form of fear is what is found in the '5' point, which is not a corner.

"But is connected to one . . ."

"Yes, as are–"

"–all the other points which are not corners!"

Her right finger jabbed at the '8' then the '1'; then, gathering speed, the '2' and the '4'.

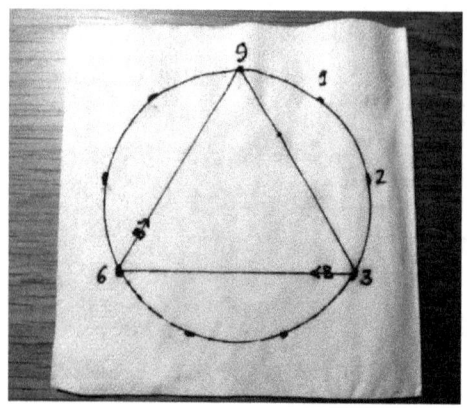

I didn't need to speak then, I just watched her get the connections, the sets of two qualities either side of each of the three corners of the core triangle.

"So the five and the seven are both variants of fear."

"Yes. the five is known, in the language of our 'sins', as avarice.

"The thirst for things - material possessions!" she looked triumphant.

"Yes, but it's the keeping of them that's the crucial driver of this point - 'stations' is the word I prefer, rather than 'points'."

"Stations, as in railway stations?" I could see this might be a step too far.

"Well, yes - any sort of station really." I replied, finishing my drink and embarking on the water.

"And there are trains?" she giggled.

Revelations do that to us - make us giggle. It's a healthy sign.

"Well, now that you–"

"–Can we come back to that?" She interrupted in a very legal way. I'm keen to know what the other point–station, related to the '6', is?"

"As in seven?" I asked.

She nodded.

"As in seven minutes past when you were supposed to be out of here?" I tapped my watch and listened to her shriek. She would still make the train, I knew - she was a very careful planner and always allowed contingency; something tightly coupled with the '7', I suspected she was; but I wasn't about to tell her that, until we met again, or maybe not for many weeks, yet.

Five minutes later, with a fresh coffee, I was still chuckling at the memory of her flying out of the door, swearing, and with two bags in one hand, the coat in the other, and her glasses wedged between her teeth . . . and looking the happiest I had seen her for years . . .

It can do that to you, the ennea-thingy.

Five

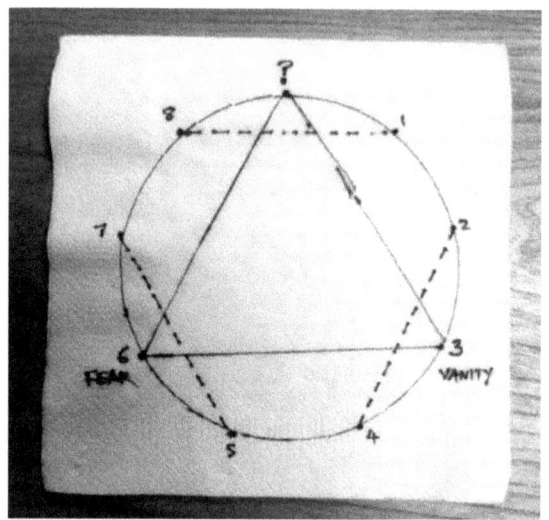

      The rain lashed at the seafront cafe's windows. Would this horrible wet weather never end? I wondered, as I hurried, slightly late because of the heavy and slow traffic, into the warm interior.

Alexandra had not wasted the extra time. Before her, on our table, lay a newly-drawn enneagram on a fresh serviette. I took off my raincoat, sodden despite the brief walk, and tried not to drip on her carefully prepared diagram.

"Coffee," she said, pointing at my cup but not looking up at my face.

"Thank you." I sat down, smiling at her relish at having the upper hand. I watched her draw in dotted lines connecting the numbers '2' and '4'; '5' and '7'; and finally, '8' and '1'.

"Shoulders . . . " I said softly into the silence of her concentration.

"Shoulders?" she asked, still looking down at the point of her pen, eager not to smudge the napkin too much.

"The lines you have just drawn – they are generally called 'shoulders'."

"Aha . . ." She looked up, finally, and put the top back on the pen. "Shoulders, then."

"So, we have nine points, which originate from three?" I asked, innocently.

"Yes," she replied, taking the bait.

I continued, "And the three – vanity, fear and something as yet unnamed, are the anchor points of the whole thing, and have other points between them, which are secondary."

We both sipped our coffees. She was looking at me in a predatory way. She'd been doing her homework, I could tell. She wanted to show it off . . .

"I'm beginning to get the big picture." she smiled. "The Nine are really only three 'sins', and these are indicative of something that we all share in our makeup?"

"I like indicative," I said, nodding and attempting to look mysterious.

"So the 'sins' are something deeper – something that has been discovered to be part of human nature, possibly all human nature?" She fixed me with a wicked smile, and continued with, "Let me guess – psychology?" You would never have guessed she hadn't just thought of it – well not unless you had known her all her life . . .

I sipped my coffee, enjoying the hunt and saying nothing.

She had never been good at waiting and filled the silence with, "And somehow these findings map on to the enneagram, which was not originally designed to show such relationships?"

"I didn't tell you that." I replied in a soft tone. "You've been reading!"

"As a good barrister should!" she parried, becoming very cat-like. But then her brows furrowed and she added, "But I can't find any link between the original work and this 'sins' stuff."

"Between Gurdjieff's original use of the enneagram and those who developed it in a different but complementary direction?" I asked, delighted with her growing knowledge; though that would now make it harder to keep her on track.

"Precisely!" she said, looking triumphant.

I spoke over the coffee cup's rim, "Connections – there isn't one, unless you count people and their individual experiences."

"People?"

"People with broad shoulders," I said, noting the time and knowing she'd be furious that I was bringing our Monday morning to a close.

She looked down at her drawing of what I had called the shoulders flanking the main three points, puzzled. It was time to give her a lot of information, but I had little time.

"Vanity and fear mix, or, put another way, what is beneath them both varies its proportions. When you move from vanity towards fear you get envy at '4' and then avarice at '5', which we've already talked about." I could see her razor mind filing this away for the train journey to London. "And between the unnamed top of the clock and vanity we have Anger at '1' and Pride at '2'. We can talk more about this next time . . ."

"And the enneagram doesn't resolve to three," I added as a kind of checkmate and tapping the face of my watch. "It resolves to one . . ."

"You–" she squeezed out the words through thin lips.

"–taxi driver, as it happens . . ."

"Taxi driver?"

"Yes, the car is outside. I didn't want you to have to walk with your heavy bags in this rain, so I stuck it outside"

"On the yellow line?"

"Broad shoulders . . ." I said, picking up two of her black bags and heading for the exit.

Six

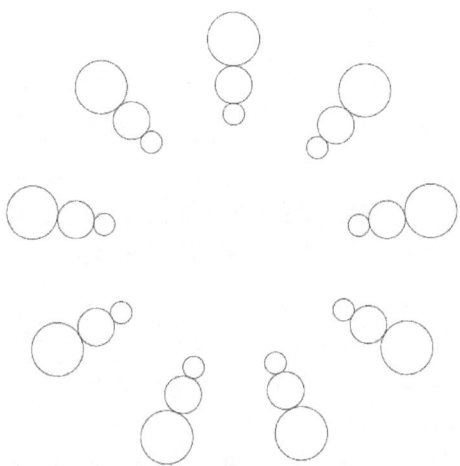

"You're not going to eat that, are you?"

I watched the tableau unfold. The rolled slice of Dutch cheese was just an inch from my mouth when she stopped me. I was grateful she had, because, in my half hour of cheesy construction, the previous evening, I had mauled it somewhat, with my fingers and my wife's borrowed cake cutters, and didn't really relish the prospect of eating my explanatory creation.

"Why not?" I exclaimed, pretending to look hurt, and letting the cheese slice unroll onto my carefully prepared napkin.

"You're not allowed to eat food not bought on the premises, dummy!"

And then she saw the unravelled slice and giggled. I love it when Alexandra giggles - she lights up a room and the relaxed behaviour is in such contrast to her normal legal manner.

"What's that?" she asked, through bouts of laughter, now so loud they were making everyone else in the coffee bar look up from their drinks.

"It's a piece of cheese full of holes," I explained innocently.

Her laughter hadn't stopped. "I can see that, but you're never that simple . . ." She sucked in some much-needed air and stopped the cackling, hissing at me, "What is it, really?" There were tears running down her cheeks.

"Well, it is a cheesy slice full of holes." I was maintaining the innocence very well in the face of her uproarious provocation.

"I can see that . . ." she took some coffee to calm herself. "Okay, you want me to decode it?" she added.

"Well if you can?"

She threatened to crack up, again, so I stepped in to help. "On one level it's a slice of cheese, which I now thankfully don't have to eat. On another level it's–"

"–A kind of enneagram." Her breathing calmed, remarkably quickly, as her razor-sharp mind focussed on the object she had so recently found hilarious. It was lovely to watch.

"Okay, Mr Cheese has brought us a circle of nine sets of holes; each hole in its set is smaller than the other, with the graduation from larger to smaller going inwards - towards the centre of the circle."

"It's a kind of cheesy perspective." I added, not being particularly helpful.

"Quite literally, by the 3D look of it?"

"Yes," I said. "There is meant to be the feeling of 'descent' in there."

"Descent from?"

"From where we are now."

She sipped some more coffee. "Oh I see, so we're at the top of a cylinder thingy, and the world" She paused again. " . . . The real world falls away beneath this upper layer, which we therefore assume has some falseness in it?"

She was stunning. "Exactly so!" I said, smiling broadly into my own coffee, so as to disguise it.

"Well let's see . . ." She was getting her teeth into it, now. "There are nine 'things' and I know that there are nine 'sins', although you - stubbornly - haven't mapped them all out for me yet!"

"Perhaps you haven't deserved it yet?" I knew that level of challenge would fire her up. "Anyway, we needed the cheesy thingy to make sense of the whole."

She sat back and looked at me, adversarially, over the rim of her cup.

"None of this is going to be easy, is it?"

"You don't like easy - you don't respect easy!" I said, with complete honesty. Her face lit up. "It's full of holes–" She finished her coffee with a giant swig. "You never waste things, so something else is full of holes–" She drank from an empty coffee mug. "–my knowledge?"

"Yes," I said. It was time to be helpful in a more obvious way. "We've darted around the enneagram on bits of paper and I've done that to let you to find our own way into it. But now we need to be a bit more structured about this truth machine."

"And now, you'll tell me what the Nine is?"

"I'm sure you've already looked it up." I said. "In fact, I'm sure your office has several books on the enneagram scattered across its leather chairs."

"But?" she asked, now taking on as much false innocence as I had ever mustered in her presence.

"But that's not the same as insight, is it?"

"No, dammit, and you know that!"

"So, when you come back to me with a real insight into what the Nine is, I'll confirm it . . ."

"And until then?"

"Until then, you're having the time of your life figuring it out!"

She was already standing, looking at her watch.

"Can we fill in the cheesy holes next week?"

"Some of them - here, you can make your own cheesy thingy!" I passed her the piece of paper I had been keeping on my knee. "It often helps to draw it; I think we can graduate from napkins, now."

With a flash of a smile, she was gone; looking as happy as I've ever seen her...

Seven

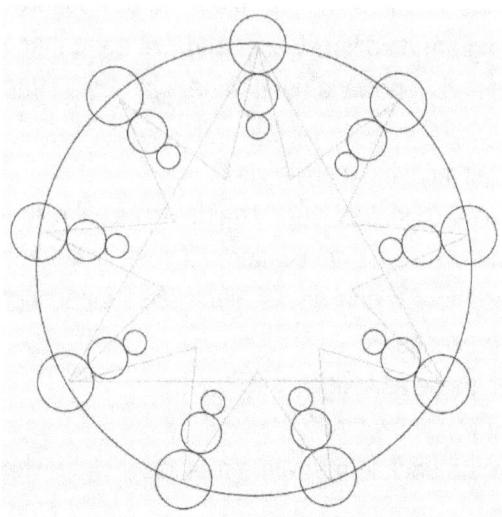

       "So the circle of stations on top of your cheesy cylinder are the outermost layer of something?"

Alexandra was in fine form. Outside the coffee shop, the first real day of spring-like weather was in full flow, despite the early hour. We had decided to celebrate this visible end of winter by sitting outside.

I had bought the coffee. Alexandra had brought us a single daffodil around which I had unceremoniously wrapped my watch. She had stared at the gesture but said nothing. The mixture of technology and nature had her bemused.

"They are, indeed, the outer layer of something," I replied, stroking my finger over the delicate edge of the daffodil's petals and marvelling at the power of the wave to put into our hands exactly what we need for that point in time.

"A bit like a flower?"

She had caught the inference. "Yes," I replied. "Just like a flower"

"And we are the flower, with all our petals being the numbers around the enneagram . . ?"

I said nothing, just nodded into her excited eyes. She had always loved the intellectual chase of such things. Becoming a barrister had simply cemented what she had always been good at.

"So the outer – upper – layer of your cheesy cylinder-enneagram is the layer of outer petals of our own flower?"

"Our own unique flower – and sometimes these flowers aren't so pretty . . ." I let that one hang, watching her digest its implications. "In fact," I added. "The enneagram is really a flower in reverse, with the most beautiful bits hidden, but otherwise sharing the same principles – the same soil, we might say!"

"Hidden?" She mused on that and sat back, sipping her coffee.

"Hidden in the way that, say, a root is . . ."

I unfolded the computer drawing I had done for her. For the first time, it had a complete list of the 'sins' in the penultimate layer of the circle. Each of what I had called the 'stations' had been filled in. Before her hungry eyes, there was now a perfect circle of information; and a set of frustratingly empty 'petals' to the outside of them.

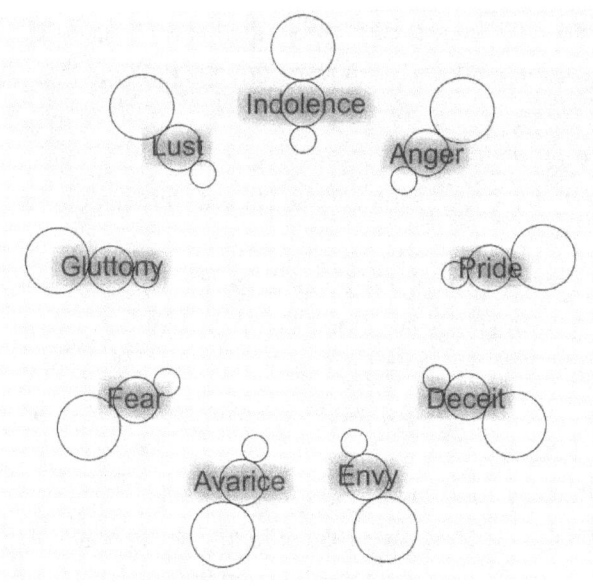

"But the sins aren't at the edge!"

"Quite right . . . that's because modern esoteric psychology has come up with an extension to the sins which gives us a great insight into how each type of person looks at the world – their own world."

She considered each of my words carefully. There were several new ideas in there, and I watched her tease apart the ends of the threads.

"Each type of person?"

"Yes, although the flowers that we are – cheesy or not – are unique, we all fall into certain types; and these particularly affect the overall way we look at the world."

"And there are nine types, I assume?"

"Exactly so, each made up of a set of reactions to our infant life."

"Infant life? So this is all about childhood?" She was leaning forward to be closer to me. The coffee was forgotten.

"Well, yes and no." I sat back and, infuriatingly, sipped some of my own coffee, before continuing, "Where this type – the outer petals of our flowers – came from is most certainly our infancy. But how we use them to get back is very much about adulthood."

She was looking at the time. There were only minutes left, and she had about a hundred questions. I could see her breathing had quickened, as she sifted what she wanted – needed – to know before she got onto that weekly train to London.

"Get back; you said get back . . ."

I nodded. She had picked on the very sentiment I had hoped she would. "Yes, get back . . ."

"To where?" She was putting her things back into her black leather handbag; watching the time in an agony of too little information.

"Where do the best signposts take any of us?" I asked, playing the most powerful card I would ever have with this lovely lady.

"Tell me . . . please?"

"Home," I said softly, looking into her hazel eyes. "Home."

She was long gone when the waitress brought me the bottle of mineral water and the small, turned wooden vase. I had spotted it, earlier, in the glass case at the back of the cafe. The owners ran a display of work for sale by local artisan painters and craftsmen; and the little vase had exactly met my immediate need.

Life is important – in all its forms, and it's always been my belief that those with intelligence have a duty to protect and nurture it.

Eight

She leaned forward, and at the same time, took a large swig of her coffee. I had seen her do it many times; it signalled that she was about to launch her enquiry.

"Home?" I asked, softly, completely ruining her build-up.

"How did you–?" she laughed, there was little sign of the irritation that would have accompanied my impolite gesture back when we first started our discussions about the enneagram.

"It's what I would have asked first, given where we got to last time."

"Uncanny!" she said, sitting back and enjoying the coffee, now that she didn't have to lead with the right question. It was hard being a barrister, her furrowed brows explained; but her smile said something different . . .

"Okay then," she added, reasonably. "Home . . ."

I drank some of my own coffee. My reply had to be perfect – not in a general sense, but in the context of our meeting. I had something unusual planned, but it required careful staging – and her full cooperation.

"The enneagram is only a symbol," I said, softly. "But it's a very beautiful expression of some wonderful truths; and their relationship." I let that sink in, drinking some more coffee before continuing. She waited and considered what I had said.

"So home is where everything begins?"

"Yes," I responded carefully, drawing out the word.

"But?" she had picked up on the hesitation.

"But, it's not like regressing, going back in our lives. It's really about taking the good stuff with us?"

"The good stuff?" Now she was looking mischievous. I could see she was enjoying this.

"There's a difference between something like skills, and other, more negative things we may have learned from life."

"Like fear?" She was being really quick, today. I had to keep her headed where we needed to be.

"Like fear, yes – but we're all afraid . . ." It was a dead-end. I knew it would leave her little to grasp at, forcing her to open it up, again. I pounced before she could.

"As different types, it's really a question of what frightens us, not whether we're frightened." I watched as she worked that apart. Her slight nodding – subconscious to her – indicated that she well understood fear.

"But fear is not primary?" she asked. "It's not that we're born with fear!"

I was there. "No," I added, speaking so low it was practically a whisper. "Fear happens when we leave home."

It took me a further ten minutes to persuade her to let me drive her to a different station. I knew that the faster London trains stopped at Oxehholme and that she would be at her destination no later than a half hour behind her usual schedule. I was banking on the fact that she would be well prepared, and have enough slack in her Monday to allow this to work. After the first few minutes she let me win, but gradually.

In the car she was relaxed. Her black bags were stowed in the ample boot and she was enjoying being 'kidnapped'. When we got to the valley she was surprised when I passed her a pair of walking boots.

"Ten minutes, I promise." I said. We began walking. As we approached the strange hilltop where I had often stood at this time of year, I diverted her attention, making her look back down the valley as we walked the final few steps to line us up with the sun, still rising over the far side of the steep hill. And then, I put my hands gently over her eyes, and turned her around to see what I had come to know as the One Tree.

There was nothing particularly special about it. It was just a tree set in an extraordinary spot. I realised I had been quite tense about the timing, but one look eastwards showed me that I need not have worried. We were right on time – we and the sun. I took my hands away and watched her focus in wonder at the tree, and then the sun behind it.

"Home," I said. Smiling at the gentle conspiracy of sun and human intent. "Sometimes there are no words for what we are trying to say". Her breathing deepened as she took in the idea behind the visual, but, magnificently, she managed to say absolutely nothing . . .

She was still holding her silence when I pecked her on the cheek and handed over the last of her bags as she got on the express from Glasgow to London.

Nine

The space between us had changed.

I smiled as I sat down next to the tall latté waiting for me in the coffee shop opposite the roaring spring sea which was doing its best to reclaim the old seaside town.

"You knew, didn't you?" Alexandra asked, in a question that wasn't. "Knew that the sun in the tree would change things?"

"I did," I replied, "But it was a hope rather than a certainty. Such things are always at the mercy of the moment."

She thought about that carefully. "Mercy of the moment – I like that . . . " She sipped a little of her own coffee before continuing. I held back so as not to disrupt the gentle flow of her thoughts and feelings.

"The moment is important in the enneagram, isn't it?"

"In the style of enneagram we use, it`s probably the most important thing" I replied, softly, putting as much flow into my voice as I could.

I looked at her face: the barrister within was fighting that quiet flowing moment, wanting to cut it apart, to dissect its intellectual content, not simply to leave it whole and approach it the way I wanted her to do. I watched as the struggle progressed and then smiled, inwardly but sadly, as the legal mind won.

"We," she said, looking me in the eye with a hawk-like stare. "You said 'we'" She didn`t notice my slight sigh – I, too, would now have to go with the new flow. "Yes, I did."

"This is a group thing?"

"Groups generate their own power in addition to the companionship they provide. Learning in a group can be very empowering. "And no," I added.

"No?"

"No, I don't want you to join a group . . ."

"Why not!?" she blurted out, unable to contain the reaction I knew would result.

To hide my urge to chuckle at the smug response I was about to give – which did not reflect my real desire, but suited the moment, I drank some of my own coffee, which, mercifully, had cooled enough to allow it. I hadn't chosen this route of discussion, but Alexandra always rises to a challenge, and the opportunity was too good to miss.

"Because you're not ready yet . . ."

There was no scream; and yet, if you knew her well, there was. A long subvocal moan with the power to shock most of the people around us. What came out was a whimper.

"Not ready . . . " She managed to keep the tone flat.

"That's right," I said calmly, pretending not to be rocking inside. "Despite the heroic efforts you have made . . ."

The inner lawyer fought for control, again, and decided there was nothing to gain down this cul-de-sac, coming at me along a different tangent. "The moment . . . tell me about the moment."

It was time to be both direct and as powerful as possible. Time was passing and she needed her seed-thought for the week. "The moment is where the real happens. It is the only place where what is real is . . ."

"What is real?" She repeated my sentiment.

"Yes. We live in a world of imagination," I said. "The age we live in has conditioned us to see reality as lots of different things – the past, the future; as though they were not merely thoughts and had some substance. Try it – reach out now and touch the future . . ."

I watched her right hand actually move, just slightly, as she wrestled with the idea of grasping the not-present.

"Yes, that idea of reaching out for a reality defined only in thought is common to us all – but I didn't say reach across the table, in space, I said reach into the future, which has no reality at all . . . though its eventual components may have a present probability"

She was silent; her thought-machine fascinated by what would, ultimately, undo it.

"Because it's a truth machine, the enneagram is centred in what is real; and the only thing that is real is now, the moment."

"And where is that on the enneagram?" she asked, returning to the flow.

"Why, it's in the centre, and radiating the wave, I replied, leaning across the small table and tapping her watch."

As I dropped her off at the station, I could see her lips forming the word 'wave' silently, as the legal mind in the background got out its scalpels and prepared to dissect it.

Her week would be an interesting one . . .

Ten

"Tell me about the 'wave'?" Alexandra asked, excitedly. "I get the idea of the now, though I think that's something we all take for granted; but the wave sounds like something to be discovered, something fundamental to existence . . ."

I sipped my coffee and looked back into those excited, bright eyes, and considered how to fill her with the sense of joy that the idea of the wave always generated in me.

I began slowly, almost hesitantly, "The wave is the substance of the now; just like the soul has been called by some the substance of consciousness." I watched as she absorbed this challenging concept. Both these ideas were seldom comprehensible to the beginner, and yet, in what the Buddhists called 'Beginners Mind', lay the simplicity of comprehension that could make great leaps through not being bogged down by the weight of accumulated thinking. To the Buddhists beginners mind was not something belonging solely to the beginner, but a state to be sought by all of us.

She sat back and drank some of her coffee. Her brilliant mind was working hard at this. Eventually, she said, "So this wave, which is the now, radiates from the centre – in this case the centre of the enneagram, giving us this moment in time, presumably, in which we can choose to live . . .?"

"We have no choice but to live on the wave, there is nothing else. The choice is whether we give it the attention it deserves and stop worrying about the phantom constructs of the process of thought." It was as direct as I could make it. I could see her reeling slightly from the mental force behind it.

She was gentle in her reply, sensing that these concepts were at the heart of what she found fascinating about our whole direction of investigation. "I can see that in our circle of the enneagram the wave originates from the centre and radiates outwards . . ." She paused, then, "But how does this relate to the character types we have been discussing on the outer rim, the Nine on the perimeter of the circle?"

It was an excellent question. Now, I had to reach into the now, my wave, and see what lay there, what could be taken at its most potent and used, with gratitude, to put more light onto the subject. Suddenly, it was in front of me – a perfect analogy for Alexandra's vast and educated mind.

"The whole of the inside of the enneagram's circle is a sea," I said, leaning forward. "Around the outside are nine islands. Parts of this sea are calm and parts of it – the outer regions – are stormy. Life sweeps us from the centre, on our own wave, to the extremities; and the journey makes us fearful and changes us."

She sipped her coffee, draining the cup, then smiled at me in a very beautiful way. "Full fathom five my father lies . . ." She winked, enjoying the allusion to The Tempest.

She had found the trail which had been in my mind seconds ago. "Perfect!" I beamed back at her. So, now, shipwrecked on a foreign island you meet–?"

She was close to giggling, again, with the excitement of real discovery. "Ummm . . . a wise old man named Prospero, his daughter, Miranda, and a beast of a man called Calaban."

She was great. The barrister's mind had retrieved the context, swiftly – doing what minds do best. I added more encouragement, "This is not specific to the enneagram, of course, but here you have a set of human characters which represent what we might call the 'levels' or centres of our lives: Prospero, the wise but impotent old man, who we could rightly say might represent the intellect; Miranda, his daughter who could be both heart and soul; and finally Calaban, the very potent but unregenerate 'savage' who is the very essence of instinct, appetite and human energy!"

"But these are not the 'types' we drew around the enneagram's circle?" she asked, certain of her ground.

"No," I responded, nodding my approval. "These are what we might call the vertical elements of each; the Nine are something entirely different – and each of them has the three levels, or centres in which their humanity – in all its vulnerability – is focussed."

"A whole cast of players . . . " she said, softly, speaking to the inner stage she had just discovered.

"Yes . . . and all unique to the wave that washed us ashore, that continues to wash us ashore, to the land of exile of our outer facing lives!"

She stood up. I looked at my watch and reached to get my raincoat – it was raining hard outside; not unusual for a Monday in May.

"No! Stay!" Her hand came down softly on my shoulder. "I need another coffee. You need to stay here and tell me more," she grinned. "In return for yours . . ."

"But your train?" I laughed at her departing back.

"To hell with the train!" she laughed, her heeled feet dancing across the cafe's wooden floor as she made her way to the counter.

Eleven

The sand was wet under our bare feet. Alexandra insisted on taking my hand and leading me into the shallow waves that lapped at the muddy beach. With her rolled-up suit trousers and my similarly shortened jeans, we must have looked quite a pair.

I looked at her and laughed, "You're doing this because I mentioned waves?"

"I'm doing this because whatever you've done, it's connected with something young in me and brought out a sense of abandon and adventure!"

In truth, I was now the one who was unprepared. "And the train to London?" I asked.

"I've disappeared," she chortled.

"Disappeared . . . as in without trace?"

"Yep!"

"They'll worry!" I added, wondering why I was obsessing about her bold actions.

"They'll be frantic!"

She began to laugh hysterically, then bent down to scoop some sea water into her cupped hands, which she proceeded to hurl at my head in an arc of salty spray. In slow motion, I watched it come towards me, my perception of the wonder of it keyed by the sheer energy of her actions, which had pushed me into that special state of heightened attention. Stilling the body's reactions, I let the essential smile light my face as the shower of liquid diamonds kissed my skin in a million tiny explosions and turned my eyes to look at her.

"What–?" she said, a second later. "What was that?" Her hands were still in front of her, dripping. She had been fully conscious of what had just happened.

"Well, you did it" I replied softly. "What do you think happened?"

"You kind of slowed down time!"

"Or perhaps stepped into the heart of time might be better?"

"Yes," she said, "Something like that."

"It's always there," I continued. "It just requires your full acceptance of the moment – the now . . . When that is done there is no time . . . just the wave, which is undistorted reality."

"And how do we give our acceptance to the *real* like that?"

In reply, I picked up an old stick, a salty remnant washed onto the beach by the powerful tides of the estuary. I used it to draw out a rough enneagram.

"To give our acceptance to the now, we have to cast off all the baggage that comes with the outer layers of the Nine."

"How–" she began, but I interrupted her.

"To do that, we have to work through them and seen how each one gives the world a perceptual and emotional tint; how the real, loving and objective world which is always present, is tainted in seeing by what our fears and reactions have taught us"

She stopped all other movements, gazing at the stick, which I was walking around the circle of the Nine, station by station. Something else in the potent now around us was calling. I turned to look along the beach, then called her over, pointing along the shore, with the sandy end of the stick. "The boat – look!"

The sailing boat lay on its side near the water line. It was still serviceable, but old and battered. "That's a bit like what life does to us all," I said. "We learn to sail the waters of life in a certain way, conditioned by the shape and size of our own little boat, which is formed by our reactions to life – our own shell."

"And separate ourselves from life's depths in the process?"

It was my turn to smile – her response had been magnificent. I nodded and said, "Yes, but the wave always adjusts the moment, the now, so that each second contains the power to give us what we most need, what we began to lose at station Nine here–" I stabbed the end of the stick into the upper point of the enneagram, watching her wince with the power of the gesture.

"When we were afraid of its awesomeness?" she asked, meekly.

I shook my head, making sure the gesture was gentle. "When we turned our back on our own true nature . . . because it hurt too much to remember what true life was like in the face of the storm that swept us out to sea . . ."

She was silent for the rest of the next hour. She was still silent as I put her on the London train, trying to brush off the last of the sand from the pin-stripe fabric of her trousers.

"We can begin next time," I said, giving her a peck on the cheek as I passed her the last of the black bags.

"Begin?"

"Begin considering each of the Nine from the unified perspective of the wave."

"Oh brave new world . . . I'd like that," she said, gently; waving and smiling like a little girl as the door beeped and closed, and the long snake of elegant metal left the station to begin its three-hour journey. The memory of the expression of innocence on her face stayed with me for the next few hours – it was a very happy sight . . .

Twelve

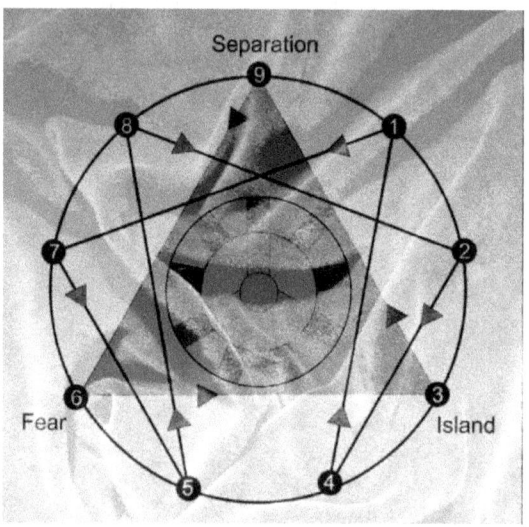

Alexandra was calmer and much more introspective when we met the following Monday morning.

"So, we're going to look at things from the unified perspective of what we have called 'the Wave'?" she said.

"Yes," I replied, taking the new drawing, from my pocket and unfolding it next to the two fresh lattes. "Examine this and tell me what you see . . ." She studied it carefully. I had arranged for it to be printed on silk so that she would treasure it.

The barrister's mind missed nothing. "The inner triangle is a different colour," she said. "And the hexa-thingy and the triangle have both been marked with arrows."

"Precisely. There are really two sequences shown in this diagram, the one made up by the sides of the triangle goes back on itself in three moves; the other follows a more complex pattern that looks a bit like a jewel." I took a sip of my hot coffee. It scalded my lips and I winced in pain.

She chortled at my discomfort, but not cruelly. "A bit like the fear reactions generated by our coming-into-the-world?" she said, still chuckling.

"Exactly so . . ." I smiled ruefully at my haste. "In our enneagram model, that would now have created a learned reaction which would stay with the developing person, forming a foundation layer on which other, more complex reactions would be layered, but, though primitive, that foundation layer would be very powerful."

"In the brain?" she asked.

"Absolutely in the brain," I replied. "Much of what is considered mystical actually takes place in the brain – though that is not to say that there isn't, alongside that, the truly spiritual."

I watched her trace the sides of the triangle from station nine to six to three; and then back to nine again. "And you said that this first move–" she re-traced Nine to Six. "Was a basic move away from our true nature – that which is really spiritual in us?"

I loved it when she used her own logic in this way, though it held a trap, since the temptation would always be to use the brain rather than what lay beyond. It was so hard for someone very clever setting out on a spiritual path to consider that the brain – the ordinary mind – was incapable of even conceiving of the spiritual life beyond the brain patterns of reaction and personality.

She continued, "So at Six we learn fear and the patterns begin to form that will become the us that the world knows, but there is something much more alive buried beneath that?"

"Yes," I said. But we don't get that to start with–in fact most of us don't get it, ever . . ."

She traced a finger from Six to Three. "So we go this way, instead?"

I smiled. It was a rewarding experience to teach one so eager and so quick-thinking. "Yes, we take our fear and our hurt and go deeper into the world, creating an island of personality at Three which allows us to get some strength and stability in the world – in our world. But its satisfaction is short lived, because we cut ourselves off from the true flow and energy in life."

"But it's not entirely a negative thing?"

"Not at all–it's an essential thing. Without it we could never have the strength nor the discrimination to look back on the basic layers of fear and begin to dissolve their power."

She looked me in the eyes; her own were beautiful hazel orbs radiating her initial grasp of the significance of all this. "This is not a trivial journey, is it?" she said, very wistfully.

"No," I answered. "But it's the only one that's real. As Jung said, 'you can construct all the beings of light you like, but until you tackle your own depths, you will never make any real spiritual progress'."

She was silent for a long time. Eventually, she said, "But you would say that there's so much beauty 'down there' that it's all worth it?"

"Yes," I said. "There's so much beauty 'down there' that it will make you cry with delight; make you feel that, as the Sufi's always said, the Beloved has returned to your life . . ."

We sat in silence for a long time, thereafter, and then I drove her to the station. With a gentle peck on the cheek she left for her other world, one increasingly encroached on by her developing spiritual awareness . . . the journey was going well.

Thirteen

Alexandra arrived to find her coffee waiting on the table; together with an old silver coin.

"It's a half-crown," I said, in response to her puzzled look. "You may never have seen one, before?"

"I have. My grandfather had some; and what am I supposed to do with it?" she asked, in reply.

"Why, you spin it, of course!" I was being irritating, but it was for a purpose, besides, I am not old enough to be her grandfather.

"One coin, two faces – okay, technically a head and a tail? So," she paused to take a breath. "What am I choosing between?"

"Much better," I was ready to drop the curmudgeon. "Between a dance around the clock or a hexawaltz!"

"A what!?"

"I just made it up – a hexawaltz . . ."

She sat down, looked at me as though she could throw something, then decided to sip her coffee. "See reaction forming, stand back, creating inner space. Let reaction play itself out in imagination . . . smile, instead." She beamed at me.

"Dammit, that was far too good," I admitted, taking some of my own coffee.

"And now the choice–as my reward, professor . . ."

"I'm not your professor, but the choice is between walking the perimeter of the enneagram or dancing the hexaflow – either way we will cover the full circle of nine stations – as I promised, and in a bit more detail this time."

"Now that I know about the wave and the context of where the Nine came from?"

I nodded. "Now that you know all that." I flicked the coin into the air above our table. "Call it!"

"Heads!" she had blurted it out before she realised that there was no outcome associated with the choice she had made. I let the half-crown fall into my palm and slapped it, opposite side down on the upper side of my left hand.

"So which way are we going to do it?" she said. "Since the coin is, clearly, irrelevant!"

"Awww, and I was having such a good time!" I said.

"I know you were – that's why I spoiled your fun!"

"Ouch!" I said. "Bested by my favourite legal mind, again . . ." I revealed the snake on the trick coin and sat there grinning and insufferable. She chuckled into her coffee.

Alexandra muttered into the froth, "Bastard . . ."

"Not entirely," I defended my stance. "There is method in the professor's madness, and probability is an important issue in the greater picture of the enneagram."

"Snake, then . . ." She sat back, crossing one elegant leg over the other and waited. "I'm waiting . . ."

"Round the clock, then," I began. "We could start anywhere, but remember that everything in the enneagram, viewed as a clock face of process, progresses from Zero to One to Three to Nine."

"Zero? You never mentioned zero before!"

She was right. I nodded, smiling.

"Zero really occupies the same spot as Nine, and marks the initiation of something for which Nine is its completion – It's similar to how Ten works in our decimal system, yet contains the One from which it began – we don't start counting at zero do we? And yet, mathematically, it's there; but of rather a different nature from One"

"Okay," she said, leaning forwards. "So a raw Zero state gets processed 'around the clock' of the enneagram to end up as the Nine at the end of the cycle."

"Exactly so–in nine stages, just like a spiral."

That idea took hold immediately. "Oh, that's good, so, it's really three-dimensional, but, because we can only see it from above, we just see it returning to Nine, as though Nine were unchanged and just the point of starting again."

"Whereas–?" I prompted.

"Whereas, really, in any process, the Nine represents what you would call an alchemical completion of a cycle . . ."

"Breathtaking!"

"Thank you." She smiled. "I do listen . . .sometimes." She chuckled, again. "When I'm not wanting to throw coffee at you!"

It was my turn to sit back and drink my coffee. "And you have to go, now, but before you do, I can tell you the exciting news that there are people living around the enneagram!"

There was mirth in her eyes. "Shock, horror–people, no less! Squatters, possibly!"

Her laughter was infectious. I joined in the mirth. "Yes, people; and, sadly, their presence there has nothing at all to do with the working out of process in the general sense that Gurdjieff taught us . . ."

"Wha–"

"It's complex; but beautiful. And it deserves a full answer or you won't get the elegant sense of it all – but there are two systems of human development alive and well in this beautiful glyph and they co-exist very well . . ."

Ten minutes later, I helped her onto the train. She leaned down to give me the customary Monday hug and peck on the cheek.

"Such fun," she said, as the carriage doors whooshed shut.

Fourteen

Alexandra was late arriving for our usual Monday morning coffee. She stormed into the coffee shop and slammed down the heaviest of her bags, making her less-than-hot latte shake in its tall glass tumbler.

"Some people," she fumed. "should never have be granted driving licences . . . that taxi-driver is one of them!"

If one can be said to sit down in anger, then she did.

"Morning," I said, neutrally, looking up from rummaging in my bag. "Pleasant weekend?" I enquired, hazardously.

"Oh stop, it," She said; the worst was, plainly, not over. "Stop being so nice! when I'm being horrible!"

I looked at her, unable to let the humour and the timing of her mental state go to waste. "We still have fifteen minutes," I said. "And what you just said shows you are, at least, conscious of your anger . . ."

"Not doing much about it, though, am I?" she sipped her coffee, finding it nearly cold, which somehow added to her self-recrimination. "Damn it . . ." she whispered, to no-one in particular.

I smiled at her, again, and took the small thermos flask out of my bag. I watched her become distracted from her foul mood, as I unscrewed the top and let the single occupant slide out, noisily, onto my waiting saucer. That drew her attention and she noticed the changed table in front of us.

"You're having tea! You always have coffee!"

"I like tea, too . . ."

She looked down at the suspicious object in the saucer. "And there's an ice-cube swimming around your saucer."

"It's for you," I said. "It relates to the first of the points on the enneagram, going clockwise from the Nine."

"Station One?" she asked, becoming fascinated with what I was doing.

I took a small file from my bag. It had a square cross-section; the sort you would use to carry out a finishing job in woodworking. I began to file down the top of my cylindrical ice cube, carving a neat cross into the top of the ice. When I had finished, it bore a passing resemblance to a bishop from a set of chess pieces.

"A chess bishop?!" she asked, examining the solitary figure in the saucer, the giggle replacing the fading anger

"Not quite, I said. "I worked out that it was the only figure I could carve, in the time available – that was close to what I wanted to create for you."

"Not a bishop then . . ."

"No, a Queen . . . "

"Is she finished?" she asked, her eyes filling with mirth at this further Monday madness.

"Nearly," I said, pouring the near-boiling water from the silver pot into the base of the saucer – creating a sort of moat around my primitive royal figure. Within seconds, it began to melt . . .

She was struggling to catch the meaning. Her mouth was open, words forming to catch the concepts she was streaming. "Ice, water, heat . . . help me!"

"The One Station, I said, "It's useful to have a figure, an icon, which helps us crystallise the characteristics of this aspect of all our personalities."

She was nodding – getting the idea, as I knew she would. "And this one is–"

"–an Ice Queen," I said. "Pristine and perfect – or would have been if I'd had a freezer and a set of proper tools in the car . . ."

She looked down at the small ice queen in my saucer, now listing to starboard as the ice melted, unevenly. "And the boiling water?" she asked.

"The anger that causes so much self-destruction. But which, sadly, goes with the package of this aspect of ourselves."

She was quiet then, realising how wonderfully life had conspired to illustrate the principle – as it so often did.

She looked at her watch. "Got to go . . ."

"Yes, but the anger has gone, too"

"Yes," she added, looking down at the saucer. "And so has the Ice Queen."

Fifteen

"I've got you an extra coffee, in a take-away cup, because I knew you were going to be late, and I'm thoughtful like that . . ."

I watched for her reaction. The word *confusion* was written across Alexandra's face. I winced, inside – this was going to be a tough one.

"But . . . but I'm not late!" she protested, looking at her watch and beginning to look irritated as she flounced into the chair.

I watched her wrestle with the conflicting emotions; I had removed the normal beginning of our Monday morning from her safe grasp, and, though she had come to expect the novel, she didn't expect the completely unknown . . .

"Arguing won't do you any good," I said. "It's important that you recognise that, although I do my best to look after everyone in my care, I make the rules; and expect those who are going to help me to do it with their fullest consideration!"

Her mouth had dropped open. "You make the . . ."

Nine, ten, I was waiting for the explosion . . . "Why you pompous, jumped up . . ." And then she saw the smile. "Bastard . . ." she added, sipping her coffee and thinking, deeply, about the nearly heated exchange. I could see her fighting to get her breathing under control.

She took several minutes to consider her next words. "Yes I do . . ."

"You do?" I asked, genuinely curious.

"I know someone just like that."

The chameleon had changed in front of her, dropping the acting and embracing the moment – one of considerable triumph on her part.

"He or she?" I asked.

"Chief clerk of our chambers, actually." her eyes narrowed as she summoned up his inner image. "Little sod, he is, but very capable – it's what keeps him there; but you're either on his team or you're the enemy!"

"For life?"

"Pretty much – he's a great believer in absolutes." she said. "He seems to think that he epitomises the perfect figure for the organisation." she smiled at a memory which obviously contradicted that . . . "But here's the thing – he gets angry with himself, as though he's constantly failing to meet his internal picture of how wonderful he should be!"

She drank some more coffee, then added, "But it's seldom his fault; just another example of how his vision is misunderstood. And then he returns to work, and usually works around the clock to beat himself up for not being infallible . . . "

"I'm so glad. You have the perfect Two . . ."

Her eyes were still locked in their internal gaze, remembering the picture of her sometime adversary.

"The perfect, Two," I said softly, again, leaning towards her, conspiratorially.

She snapped out of her reverie. "The Two! Oh yes, I'd forgotten that we were up to the Two!"

"Let's call him Will Faul." I said. She laughed at the name.

"Okay, Will Faul it is, so what do I do with him?"

"We'll come to the remedials when we know them all a bit better." I said. For now, just study the people you meet and see how many of them fit into this profile.

"What's at the heart of a Two?" she asked. "Can't you give me a keyword, or something?"

She was looking at her watch. I knew our time was almost up and wanted to give her something in return for the rough ride.

"Okay," I said, draining my own drink. "It's all about image."

"Image," she said wistfully, already working on the ramifications of the answer. "And that's all I get?"

"That's all you need," I smiled. "For now."

She smiled back, her composure had returned. "Bloody good job we did all that prep or you'd be driving back wearing coffee!"

"Brought my mac," I said, tapping the summer raincoat behind my chair and beaming with a huge grin that spilled over into laughter.

"It's all about trust, isn't it?" she said, returning my smile.

47

I didn't reply immediately. I just stood up, nodding, threw the mac over my shoulder, and bent down to kiss the top of her head. "Yes," I whispered. "And that you know it, so soon, is beautiful . . ."

Sixteen

I had arranged to meet Alexandra on the seafront the next Monday morning. I explained that I would bring us take-away coffee, as I wanted to use the half-hour to do a large-scale drawing. I had hinted that additional footwear might be required and she looked quite incongruous when she arrived, in pin stripe suit and walking boots . . .

"Only for you!" she shouted into the gathering wind. Her smile was infectious. I winced at what I had to do. I held up the coffee and she took hers. I pointed at the beach. "We have to go down onto the sand."

She nodded, "I had a feeling it was going to be something like that!" But she followed, willingly, down the old concrete steps and onto the golden sand. Each of us took care not to spill coffee from the fragile paper cups.

I was dressed in jeans and summer boots. She looked like someone you wouldn't expect to find on a beach, early on a Monday morning. I looked at her, holding her eyes, then began to circle her, in a predatory fashion. At first she giggled and turned to her coffee for succour; but when I carried on my actions, and she was faced with something she didn't understand, she began to look less sure of herself. I continued to circle her like a wolf, my footsteps marking a rough circle in the sand.

She broke free from my tracks and headed towards the water line, where tiny waves were lapping onto the beach. Behind them, larger waves with white horses were building on the stiffening breeze. I smiled at the turn of events; feeling the warm wind turn gusty, and watching it blow at her hair and clothes, as she stood, trapped between the sea and my advancing but still silent figure. She turned away from me, drinking her coffee, a small act of the known, the familiar.

I came level with her, then studied the sea, before walking into it.

"What!" I heard her gasp, "I hope you don't think–"

But my actions cut her off, as, now up to my ankles in sea water, and sporting wet and uncomfortably splashed jeans, I began to walk a perfect segment of a circle, passing her with a still silent look, on the seaward side, before coming out of the water to complete the circle on the dry sand, dragging my feet to ensure the perimeter was clearly delineated. When I had finished, most of my circle was on the dry beach, but the final arc was submerged.

She looked at my madness. The normal humour in her eyes was gone. "Circles?" she shouted, angrily. "Is that it? Are you trying to teach me about bloody circles?" But she did not move from the spot.

Still I said nothing. It was difficult. I knew the tension was becoming unbearable and I was not doing this to be cruel. I walked to a nearby, rocky section of the beach, put down my coffee and picked up three, large pebbles. I carried them back to where she was standing, looking at her newly-insane friend, and placed them at three of the cardinal points of the circle made from my wet footprints.

Only the invisible point in the sea remained unmarked.

My feet squelched as I did so, and I, too, was acutely uncomfortable. I retrieved my coffee, which was still untouched. I looked at her angry and somewhat frightened face.

"Don't move from the circle," I said. "You're safe there."

She shouted back at me, "Safe from what, you idiot?"

I began to walk around Alexandra's safe circle, again. "Safe from me . . ."

I let the words hang in the wind.

Stunned at my response, she stood, mute in the centre of her safe prison and watched as I walked back into the sea, stopping when I was at the far point of my symbolic creation.

It must have looked surreal.

She stared at me in silent rage, then cursed as her half-full coffee cup fell from her fingers and splashed all over her safe sand. She bent to pick up the cup, but stopped. The rules of the world had gone to hell, what did it matter?.

"Walk towards me," I said, gently.

"Into the bloody sea–in my best legal suit?"

"Yes."

I watched her conduct the greatest inner fight of our friendship; watched as the past months flashed before her eyes and she reviewed the kindly outcomes of each encounter. Sometimes bodies speak much louder than the mind ever can; trust triumphed and she hung her head and walked towards the sea.

When she arrived at the water line, her head still bowed, she was surprised to find two wet and booted feet standing there. I had come forward, silently, to meet her halfway – and halfway was the water line.

She looked up. There were tears in both our eyes. I held out my full and untouched cup of coffee. "For you," I said, simply.

I cleared my throat, then said, "That's what it feels like in the land of the Enneagram's three point." I shook my head in a beloved memory of my own journey. "And what it feels like when people love you enough to pull you out of it . . ."

Seventeen

I waited while she brought the coffee; waited and moved my feet around in the sodden boots, enjoying the effect the squelching noise had on those on the next table. Eventually, she returned, smiling at my continued noise-making.

"Stop it – you're just being bad for the sake of it!" she scolded.

"I'm only human." I said, wetly.

"Thank you . . . "

I looked up into those now-gentle eyes. "Thank you?"

She sat down and sipped her coffee, assembling what she wanted to say.

"Thank you for being the person who shocked me awake on the beach;" she glanced at the shoreline across the road. "Who stalked me like an idiot, in front of the watching world, to make a wonderful and illustrative point." More coffee, then, "Who waded into a cold sea and made me see that these numbers on a circle are really vivid and imprisoning ways of seeing the world."

"Well, yes," I said, amazed and mollified at the strength of feeling. "That's a very good description."

"And they all have this, the numbers – the Types?"

"They all have their own flavours of this – though the original anticlockwise wave of the outgoing three are the anchors for the rest."

"The Nine, where it begins, the Six and this–" she looked wistfully at the beach, again. "The Three."

"Yes," I said, smiling at her infectious good spirits. "I used the Three for this increase in 'volume' of your experiences for a very good reason." I watched as she cocked her head to one side, studying me.

"You're a three?" she asked, smiling.

"Yes, I'm a Type Three." I replied.

"But you're not just a Type Three?" she asked.

"No-one is just any single type. We all have them all, so to speak, they are the story of the unfolding human . . ."

"Just in differing proportions?"

"Exactly so, according to our formative reactions – and we are all unique, though we all share some characteristics we'd rather not confess to – notably the 'sins' we began these conversations with!"

Alexandra chuckled. "Oh, yes." she whispered into the foam on her latte. "I can see that now." She drank from the mug, then asked, "So, where next?"

"Next, at least clockwise, would be the Four . . ."

"Given that I have to catch one of the London trains today, can you give me a few gems to consider in the week ahead?"

I drew in a breath and opened the moment to the right words. "You must go forward from here with what you know. You know that each of what we might call the 'Outcast Triad' – the Nine, the Six and the Three – all the same child of the divine – were stages in the One Life, the One Consciousness, the result of a turning away from our original, spiritual nature – which, in one sense, leaves it self-important, an island of safe isolation, where it can make its own rules; and . . . colourless."

I watched and drank coffee while she considered this. She took her time. Eventually, she said, "And the Three, in a sense, is where we end up – unless we carry on back to the Nine?"

"Very much like that," I agreed. "So tell me, in your own words, what that process of becoming an outcast, an exile, is . . ."

She thought for a while, then drew in a breath to speak. I leaned across the table and placed a gentle hand on her wrist, shaking my head.

"My train?" she asked, smiling.

"No, my wet feet – but you have some thinking to do for next time." I drained my coffee.

There was the happiest of silences as she walked, and I squelched, back to the car park by the sands. My boots were unlikely ever to be the same, again – but it had been worth it.

Eighteen

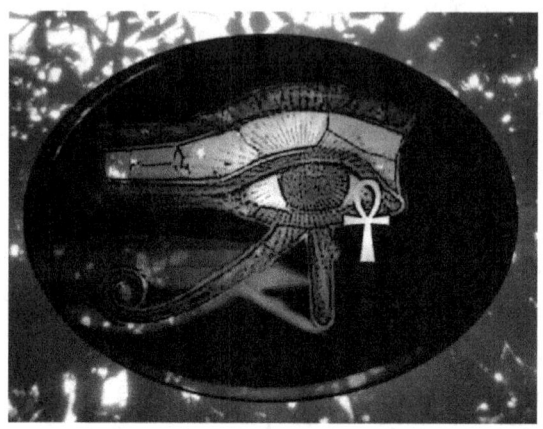

Alexandra joined me at exactly half past eight, smiling. She took a thin and exotic-looking notes folder, bound in black leather, from her large travel bag. From the folder, which she opened and laid out on our coffee table, she took a shiny, black and gold Mont Blanc pen.

"Nice . . ." I said.

"Morning!" she responded.

"Still nice . . ."

"It's kind of expected in the echelons of the legal profession," she said, leaning forward to emphasise the point. "To operate with a good-looking set of tools."

"That's it?" I asked.

"What?"

"That's all you have to say about having the best pen I can think of, and an exotic leather folder to match?"

She sat back, stretching out her arm to take her coffee from beyond the black leather object in question, never taking her eyes from my grim face.

"Did we have a bad weekend?" she asked, quite reasonably.

"I can't speak for 'we' but my wife and I had a lovely weekend." I responded, flatly. "Did 'we' have a good weekend?"

She refused to rise to the bait. "Derek and I had a great time, largely prompted by my being in a wonderful mood that continued all week from the last time we did this!" She folded her crossed legs, sideways, and retreated. "Well, not quite this . . ."

"Derek?" I said. "Did I know about Derek? Some young and clever sod from another law firm, I take it?"

There was anger, now. "Well, now you come to mention it – double first from Oxford, rich parents, but despite all that . . . a lovely man."

"You forgot young . . ." I said.

Ice. "And young . . . about half your age, if you must know."

I let the silence build to an intolerable level, watching as she pretended to lose herself in drinking coffee, writing the time, date and what was probably the word 'bastard' in shorthand on the top of the blank page.

"I never could master shorthand." I said.

"Would you like me to return some of the time you're spending on me with some lessons?" she said, looking for a way back. "I could teach you one of the easier forms of speedwriting if you'd like something simpler."

"I'd just mess it up," I said. "But it's lovely to watch you doing it so well." I held her eyes as I said it, letting the slightest flicker of a smile play around the edges of my mouth. "Would you write something else for me so that I can see the grace of the movements, again?"

She was wary. "If you like; what?"

"Write: 'this is how'," I watched the words emerge from the fluidity of her actions. "'The Type Four moves from admiration, to the melancholic consideration of what he knows he will never be able to achieve, despite it being the ideal for him . . . to the generation of hatred at the object of his jealousy in a contest that he knows is lost from the start'." Half way through, she got it, and began to swear, sub-vocally; but, disciplined soul that she was, she carried on, until every word lay on the page, written in time, space and consciousness.

At the end, we both said nothing. There was a tear in her left eye.

"Didn't think you'd be able to do that, again", she said.

"What?" I had an idea what she meant but wanted her to say it.

"Catch me off-guard like that – generate so much bloody emotion on a coffee table!"

"I didn't, not really."

"Then how–?"

"I don't plan these. I just turn up and open us to what is present . . . in the hope that what happens will convey some of the vivid sense of it all."

"Open us to the–" she looked around, at the pen, the folder, the expensive pad . . . and the coffee cup, now nearly empty. "– to these things?"

"No," I said, gently. "To *the arranger* . . ."

"The arranger?"

"Yes," I said. "The arranger of these things in our experience and in a way that lets something flow through them."

She shook her head, letting the last of her anger dissipate. "Type Fours?" she said.

"Need a lot of help, especially from Type Threes, who can understand them really well, though find them incredibly frustrating – and Type Ones, on whom they dote."

She took the cue, "The Type Two, Three and Four all sharing the same corner of the enneagram?"

Right on the nose. "Yes," I said. Each of them concerned with the image of themselves in the world. The Four being full of pride and ego-inflation; the Three being the master of the get-it-done self-centric; and the Four being the 'green with envy 'I'll never be good enough' epitome of doom."

I drained the last of my coffee and stood to go. "Coming?" I said, looking at my watch.

"When I've written this up," she said, curtly. Repaying me, handsomely. "You go . . ."

I turned to leave. She caught me with the words, just before I reached the door, "Buy you one for your birthday?"

"A Mont Blanc?" I asked, turning back and smiling at her.

"Yes," she softened. "If you really want one – if you promise you'll use it?"

"Two," I said, holding up fingers and catching a final surge of the moment, almost a sigh on the wind, like the slow-motion image of a tennis ball hitting the sweet spot on a racket for that winning point.

"You don't need two," she said. "That's greedy."

"Not for me – the second one."

"Then who?" she asked, puzzled.

"For Derek, of course . . . from you, but with my apologies for abusing his persona."

She was laughing, the tension sliding from her with the relaxed movements of her shoulders. "It's his birthday next week – you couldn't possibly have known that."

"I didn't . . . that wasn't the important thing."

As the glass door swung shut, I could still see her at the table, chuckling; fingers clutching black and gold; and flashing with speed as she wrote. At the limit of my vision, they waved.

Nineteen

Alexandra was picking her way along the shoreline at the edge of the bay, probably cursing me. She was clutching a printed copy of the email I had sent her, asking that she bring sensible footwear – for which, these days, she read 'boots' – and allow a little extra time. The note closed with my offer of bringing the coffee.

I had a short time remaining before she would find me. I closed my eyes and summoned up 'Rocky' – my short name for the Silent Eye's archetype of point five of the 'outer rim' of the enneagram. Along with Sue and Stuart, I had developed these figures of the mind to illustrate the dominant principles of the outward-facing aspects of the nine-pointed 'truth machine'.

Not that everyone wanted to know the truth . . . you had to learn to love it for its own sake; for the stony path could be sharp and painful to tender feet shorn of their usual worldly footwear. But the School wasn't about comfort, though we didn't seek, deliberately, to be without it; it was focussed on those determined souls who wanted to dig into the fertile soil of their own lives . . . and see what else might be capable of growing there.

Alexandra was in an unusual position: she could have simply enrolled as a student and studied via the Silent Eye's correspondence course, but my partners in the School judged circumstance to have brought her and (collectively) us together – and that allowed direct teaching, via our brief meetings.

I looked back along the beach trail to where she was rapidly narrowing the gap between us. She still couldn't see me, which was part of the setup; though I could view every step of her progress. Soon, she stood below my rocky perch at the end of the path, staring out at the retreating tide and looking bewildered.

"Ahem!" I coughed from above, in what I hoped was a friendly fashion.

She smiled and looked up, "Oh you're there – being a Type Five, no doubt!" She gazed up at me, watching me admire her intellect.

"Well, yes, actually . . . so, since you seemed to have grasped my methods, tell me, from what you see, something about fives . . ."

She looked up. "I'm looking up at you," she said. "So there's got to be something about position in this? – I know, you've placed yourself above me, using your knowledge of this place."

"And why would I do that?" I asked. "Am I preventing you from coming up here, too?"

Alexandra examined the short and steep path that would reunite us, but then noticed that I occupied the only natural seat at the top of the scramble.

"Hmm," she said. "No, but the path is. Not much chance of sharing a coffee up there!"

"So, I've located myself above your world, in a singular position, is that it?"

She scanned the rock, again, looking for clues in the rucksack I had set down on a ledge in the dark rock, just to the side of me. She found none.

"Are we having coffee at all?" she asked, reasonably, still digesting the tableau.

"You not only covet my high and secure place, you want to have some of my coffee, as well?" I made it sound as accusatory as possible, though I was starting to grin by the time the words were out.

I pressed home the point, knowing it would leave me bordering on 'Mr Nasty', again, "Why should I share some of my hot coffee with you?" The dual assault of isolation and meanness looked like it had begun to irritate her.

Rejecting that road–so recently endured, she took a breath and triumphed by laughing at the situation. "Okay," Another deep breath. "So you're frightened of me," she said. "So frightened that you don't even want to open that flask and share some coffee – something that would bring us closer together and make you share more than just the coffee."

"Ouch . . ." I said, softly, feeling Rocky's control of the moment slipping away. She smiled up at my crumpled face, taking fuel from her growing triumph. "You want to be separate from the world. You want to keep everything you've got!" I smiled and her face burned with the truth of that revelation. "You're a Fear Type, and your reaction to fear is to shore up your massive mistrust of the world – your world – by locking yourself away in a clever place from which you can engage with the world just as little as you want to . . ."

She was breathless. I looked proudly down on her flushed and breathless face. Then, she did something uncharacteristic – she crouched, cat like and scanned the rock face, looking for footholds and talking to me in a hypnotic way, as though fixing her prey with the words.

"In doing this, you keep the world from doing what it does best . . . evolving you!" She sprang at the rock face. I had started to slide off my rocky seat, to rejoin her below, but now, she was coming at me like a tigress. It was my turn to freeze, as, like a professional climber, she scaled the vertical distance between us and forced herself into the space that was only secure for one.

"My turn," she said, triumphantly. "My turn to play the force of Life . . ." She reached for the flask, then, with one arm completely around my middle, she held onto me while she poured the coffee, forcing me to brace us both against the stone to avoid a painful tumble.

For the next few minutes, we stayed like that, until the small coffee cups were drained, and my cramping muscles could take no more. The contact was both impersonal and full of life-force… the vitality of two people working together at depth.

Some time later, we walked back along the edge of the sand. I didn't need to say anything at all. She had risen above the world of reaction and found a jewel of real action in the moment; and she and I both knew that the world would never be the same again . . .

Twenty

       I met Alexandra at the local station. She had agreed to spend an hour longer with me before getting the London train from Oxenholme, which serves the Lake District and has a direct link to the capital. She changed into her summer boots at the back of her car, and we walked the short distance to the local bakery, which had a tiny cafe, with excellent coffee. Grasping two tall take-away cups, we sat down on the metal chairs at the open front of the busy shop.

"Six," she said. "I feel like we've been headed for type six for a long time?"

"Yes," I replied, wondering how this would open itself out. "Six is the second most fundamental unfolding of the whole enneagram – from a personality or ego perspective, anyway."

"And it has to do with fear?" She had been reading. That was no surprise, of course, but I knew that few books on the enneagram approached the topic from a truly spiritual perspective.

I sipped my hot coffee and burned my lip. "Ouch! – that will have to wait, possibly till we're down by the gorge."

"Gorge! I'm dressed for chambers, not mountaineering . . ."

"Don't worry, there's a road runs right by it." I said. "A short scamper down through the forest and we'll be on the flat limestone."

I could see she was less than convinced. She had begun to fold the paper napkin that came with the coffee into a simple plane. I suspected the action was unconscious.

"Can you make boats, too?"

She looked at me, strangely, then down at her hands. "Yes," she said.

"Will you make us one each?" I handed her my napkin and watched as her skilled fingers made light work of two small boats. They wouldn't last long, but that suited my purposes.

Fifteen minutes later we were standing by the river Kent, having just crossed it on the old footbridge that swayed as you walked its suspended length. She was still smiling from the rather scary experience; the Kent was quite wide at this point, and the water flowed slowly, gathering its forces for what was to come.

"This isn't a gorge," she said, looking around at the flat meadow with cows in it.

"That's part of the fun." I nodded. "You will be astonished how quickly the landscape changes."

"A bit like life and the unexpected?" She was fishing; and cleverly.

"Exactly like that. Got the boats? – it's time to release them into time . . ."

She took both of them out of the small rucksack she had taken to bringing when we met up for our 'Monday madness' as she termed it. "You're wearing the wellingtons, I assume you're going to launch them?"

I took the two small, paper boats and waded out as far as I could into the stream. Soon, the two boats bobbed away on the slow current.

"What now?" she asked, beginning to giggle.

"We run like fury!" I replied.

Seconds later, we raced across the old bridge like idiots, driving it to a frenzy of vibration. I could hear her hooting laughter as we charged up the small country lane before diving down under the fence and coming to a a halt at the edge of the limestone gorge.

"Wow!" she was breathless and still laughing, but astonished at the change of scenery.

"Wouldn't think they were so near each other would you; the meadow and the gorge?"

Just then, I began to point upstream, to where two tiny white boats, half submerged, were about to enter the churning water of the torrent that fed into the gorge below. For a second we stared at them, before they were spun and sunk by the violent water, slipping past us a pale shadow of their former shape. Soon, they were gone. I took the coffees out of my shoulder bag. I had packed a cup holder and they were still relatively intact, if a little cooler.

We stood and sipped the coffee. "Shouldn't we be sad?" she asked.

"What, choose to be sad?" I asked, smiling at her. "We're having a perfectly lovely summer morning watching tiny boats swirl to their doom in the white water; why would we choose to be sad?" I paused a while, then said, "It would be like choosing to be fearful . . ."

Alexandra was looking perplexed. "But, isn't that the point, that, in real life, the tragedy would be much more serious?"

"Of course," I smiled. "But even then, the perspective we need is the one of the two people on the bank of life, watching the inevitable and drinking coffee and being happy – because to do anything else is just choosing sadness . . ."

"Little people on the boats would have been terrified?" she queried.

"But only when the water became a torrent – until then, they would have been enjoying a pleasant sail on a summer's day."

She finished her coffee. "I'm going to have to think about that," she said, handing me the empty cup. "Can we carry this on next week – and come back here?"

"Of course," I replied, taking her arm and escorting her up the muddy slope and to the car.

Twenty One

We were sitting by the river, though earlier than usual. The padded plastic-bottomed picnic blanket I had brought serving us well as a coffee base on the cold limestone, which was constantly made wet by the spray from the rapids in the adjacent river Kent. Neither of us seemed to mind the gentle mist. The thermos flask had been half emptied and we were enjoying our coffee. We talked, gently. To anyone passing over the nearby bridge, we would have looked a strange pair – Alexandra in her legal suit, albeit with walking boots; and me in jeans and summer tee-shirt.

The mood was gentle, too. Fear, the central characteristic of station six on the enneagram of personality, was not a topic to which we needed to add much drama: it had enough of its own.

"We are all afraid," I said. "It's just a matter of degree and what frightens us, most. But fear has a very special spiritual role to play for us, as well."

She sipped some coffee, resting herself on one elbow. "And choice?" she asked. "You indicated last week that we choose a lot of our own fear . . ."

"Yes," I considered my next words carefully. "We are really like a native American totem pole, one where the different figures are layered on top of each other." I thought about that concept, and wondered whether that had been the original meaning of such sculptures. I dimly remembered other people having written about the idea. The lower figures would be nearer to the world of instinctive reaction – that which keeps us alive, certainly; but that which restricts the processes of higher thought and emotions until we have enough experience, and, later, trust, to build something greater on that hilltop. I pointed to a coiled length of old rope, lying half in the shallows of a quiet pool, well back from the torrent.

"Take that harmless snake over there," I said. The rope was discoloured from its long journey downstream, and covered in enough green algae to look like a convincing, and quite large, grass-snake. I knew it wasn't of course; but only because I'd been here with Tess, our collie, many times.

I could feel Alexandra tensing, even though I had said it was a harmless snake. "It's not, is it – a snake, I mean?"

"We could go over and see?"

"We could, but I'd rather you tell me that it wasn't!"

"But then you'd be relying on my reality, my experience; and not investigating your own."

"Which is how most fear starts," she whispered into the mist, standing up on legs that weren't completely steady. I watched with growing admiration as she took two steps nearer to the possible green reptile. "I'll go," she said, half-turning back to look at me. "But will you hold my hand just in case I freeze?"

"Gladly," I said. "I just won't do anything to interfere with the vividness of your experience." I stood and took her proffered hand. Together, we walked across the wet limestone. I could tell to the second the point at which her snake became an old rope. Her muscles unsnapped, fluidity returned to her body, and she began her customary laughter; but, this time, without the retributions. "Did you know?"

"Yes. Didn't think I'd expose you to a real snake, did you?"

"I didn't know for sure . . ."

"Precisely – and in that authentic unknowing you became totally present to the moment, and explored it with power."

She nodded. Pleased to have done this so well.

"Given that it wasn't a snake," I continued. "What were you frightened of?"

"What, who . . ." she mouthed, driven on by my relentless questions. She snapped her head up, straightened her back, and looked down on the rope. "Well, there were only three players – you, me and the old green rope." She was still laughing – something we all do after an attack of fear. "And I'm not known for being frightened of old bits of rope; so It must have been me!" she said.

"Exactly," I replied, "And there is a name for being frightened of ourselves, and that is anxiety. I paused to let it sink in. "Real fear – fear in response to a danger that is present, often has its own resolution built in to the problem. The brave bit is to see the problem fully, and therefore to be fully conscious to it;

if possible, with no reaction at all – which I admit is easier said than done; but that shouldn't stop us trying . . ."

"And the spiritual side of all this?" she asked

"All the inner traditions speak of a final act of coming face to face with fear, itself – not fear of an object – as the last act before a significant degree of illumination is given . . ." I paused before adding, "And remember that fear belongs only to the world of the ego, the personality – it has no place in the world of Being.

"And the importance of point six in all of this?"

"The dweller at point six, which we view in the Silent Eye as The Fugitive, is one whose life is lived on a volcano of fear, yet who is amazingly loyal and brave in action."

"Sounds almost sacrificial?"

"Well, yes, in many ways, that's how I view it, too, though the many excellent text books on the subject don't dwell on that. Within the Silent Eye, we like to keep alive the ancient and magical ideas on such subjects, so I would say that sacrifice is a good concept to use, here . . ."

Twenty Two

We ran through the steepening streets of the town. I pulled at Alexandra's wrist and, every few strides, looked around, anxiously, in search of our pursuers.

"What are we running from?" she laughed, behind me, now well used to my craziness. I had noticed that she had recently taken to wearing more casual clothing for our teaching encounters, and suspected that her larger bag, now safely in the car, contained a change of clothes or two – including a choice of outdoor footwear . . .

"I can't tell you, exactly, the image is fading, but I know it frightened me – and it's big!"

"Big?" she gasped, her voice was getting hoarse with the effort. "Big, as in an animal?"

I pulled her on, ducking and diving into the warren of alleyways that make up the Fellside district of Kendal. Fellside is a steep part of town, true to its name, that rises from the town centre and climbs south-westward up the nearby ridge. The old and narrow stone streets were perfectly suited to my purposes, and we could have been on a film set.

"It could be an animal!" I shouted, turning another tight corner and shouting in response to her previous question. "In fact, I can imagine many describing it that way; but I think it's bigger than that!" My breath was rasping in my throat, too. The gradients of Fellside were a killer.

Alexandra ground to a halt and shook free of my hauling hand, slumping forward with hands on knees. "Idiot!," she laughed. "You're killing me!"

"But, it might catch us!" I managed, weakly, between gasps, fighting hard to suppress a grin.

"It can eat me if it likes," she said, recovering her breath. "I'm not running another step . . . and I'll need a second bloody shower, now, you nuisance–"

she gasped some more. " . . . and that will have to wait until London!"

"Aww . . ." I said. "Would a coffee help make it up to you?"

She pulled herself vertical and managed a smile. "It might . . . if it's a good one."

Five minutes later, and with the cool summer breeze bringing us back to normality, I walked her – downhill, at last – to the outdoor cafe in the middle tier of the three layer mound that forms the bedrock of the Brewery Arts Centre, itself set into the lower slopes of the Fellside district. We sat on the second of the terraces in the sunshine, facing down the slope. We ordered a bottle of water each, and two large lattés. By the time they had arrived, she was speaking to me, again.

"Is this near the station?" she asked. "I have to be going, soon."

"No, but it's very near the Head."

"The Head?"

"The Sleeping Head – what we've been running from . . ."

"I don't know the–"

"Yes, you do, but it's better seen in a way that makes an impact."

For the next few minutes I said nothing else. We drank our coffees in pleasant silence, as the inner tension mounted. Eventually, I took her hand again, pulling her to her feet. "Will you close your eyes for me?"

We had come a long way in the months we had been working together. It was marked by the trust and the ease with which she accepted the request. She nodded, and I guided her, blind, up the stone staircase that had been behind us all along.

When she was safely on the upper level, I turned her to face our destination and asked her to open her eyes.

She made a slight gasp.

"This is what we all run from, when we are being the Type Six," I said, as her hazel eyes opened wider and she took in the carved head before us.

"Sleeping?" she whispered.

"Sleeping to our spiritual nature, which is actually the characteristic of the Nine, the core and start-point of the enneagram. Our life is not our reality, and so we live in a dream. This is what the Six embodies – someone whose fleeing life is the result of being turned away from its reality; from its inner trust, which it had and lost at station Nine . . . and so now lives in the land of fear; believing it is supported by nothing . . ."

Twenty Three

We met at our usual coffee shop on the seafront–it having become anything but usual over the past few weeks; when our short, Monday adventures had taken us out in the landscapes around the bay.

"Ah, normality! – So, at least I'll get to London on time," said Alexandra, sitting down at the table and looking glad to be enjoying a less hectic Monday morning. "My partners in crime were beginning to doubt my continued excuses . . ."

"Ah, yes . . . normality . . ." I said, looking up, just as our coffees were brought over. We often collected them from the counter – Monday morning being a busy time for the small cafe. "Thank you." I said, looking up at the lady delivering our drinks. "And the Danish pastries?"

"Be right along – haven't forgotten them!" replied Rose, brusquely. She was the elderly owner of the place. She marched back to the wall of glittering machinery beyond the counter. The old building had retained a kind of untidy Art Deco charm and was stocked with some of the most ancient-looking espresso machines I had ever seen – one of the reasons we loved it so much. I watched Alexandra as she sipped her hot and frothy latté, looking very happy with life. "A quiet Monday and Danish? I am being treated!"

"Richly deserved," I said, savouring my own hot, milky drink.

Just then, Rose, returned, carrying a tray; containing, not what Alexandra was expecting, but another two lattés. Alexandra looked at them, suspiciously, and seemed about to speak.

I intercepted, quickly. "They've introduced a new hazelnut syrup – it's delicious," I said, continuing to drink my existing coffee, noisily. "I know you have a sweet tooth and thought you might like to try it?"

"Well, that's very kind, but . . ." The confusion was visible on her face. Before her, now, were two coffees. "Do we have time?" she asked, plaintively.

Rose's second arrival, with six Danish pastries, occurred a second later, and perfectly on cue. This was going to cost me, I thought, and not just in breakfast funds . . .

"Six!" blurted out my companion, spraying the froth from her coffee across the table top as she surveyed the growing excess of food and drink. "We'll never eat three each, they're huge!"

"But they're baked to one of Rose's new recipes . . . and they are absolutely gorgeous!"

"I don't care how wonderful they are," Alexandra said, looking forceful. "I can't possibly do justice to this tableful of . . ."

She broke off. "It's the seven, isn't it?" she snarled, already beginning to laugh at the chaos before her. "It's the bloody seven!" She coughed, some of the froth lodged in her tightened throat. "Don't tell me – gluttony!"

"Of course," I replied, gently. "We met it briefly, before, on our cursory initial look at the enneagram, but you weren't involved with it then . . ." I look at the overburdened table top, smiling ruefully. "Now you've no choice!"

She sat back, looking calmer, sipping her original coffee. Her taut body language suggested she was going nowhere near the rest. "Too much of everything? – The Type Seven behaviour?"

"Yes," I said. "Too much choice, too much selection, too many things on the go, too many projects . . ."

"And all impossible to do justice to?"

"Exactly"

"I know lots of people like that . . ."

"Me too." I said. "Why do you think people do this? Think where it is on the enneagram . . ."

"It's still in the 'fear' corner, centred on Station 6, yes?"

"Exactly."

"So what's he frightened of, our Mr Seven?"

"You tell me." I said. "It's all there – in her behaviour . . ."

She sat back and became very thoughtful. Sipping the coffee. "He gathers – everything. He stockpiles it all, but, unlike Mr Five, he's less concerned about 'keeping' it than acquiring more and more . . ."

"Very good." I was not being patronising – that had truly been an excellent

72

analysis of this aspect of human experience.

"And all this is driven by the basic fear that . . .?"

"That the world won't feed us, in every sense of the word."

"And therefore a complete lack of . . .?"

"Trust in our own lives; and the fortune that actually shines on us all. We fill our lives with too much because we are frightened; and in turn the excess makes us choked of freshness, miserable and more frightened . . ."

She looked at her watch and stood up, surveying the scene, and ready to head for the rail station. Rose arrived with a small army of pastry bags. "You'll be needing these, I take it," she said, looking daggers at me. "And the bill?"

I nodded into Rose's accusing eyes. I had been a regular for a long time, but this behaviour had been stretching it a bit. "Yes, please," I said. "But I think the bill is the least of my worries . . ."

When it came, the amount did make me wince. Alexandra, who would have enjoyed the moment, was long gone, though I could hear her chortling over the airwaves . . . Danish for lunch, I thought.

Twenty Four

I sat, nervously sipping my coffee, wondering where Alexandra was. It was 08:45 and she should have arrived at least fifteen minutes ago. I was on edge for two reasons: firstly, I was worried that a woman who was never late should be so, now; secondly, an honest description of that part of our mental and emotional make-up that was the enneatype eight was difficult territory, and its explication had come close to costing me several friendships in the past! I had been tense entering the cafe, over half an hour prior – now I was positively anxious!

08:50, and my unease was being compounded by the vivid conversation from the woman sitting behind me, whose perfume happened to be maddeningly attractive. I dared not turn around but I couldn't help tuning in to the animated conversation with someone I took to be her partner on the other end of the mobile phone call.

"Well, I bet you would! The last time you proved how right you were, you sneered for a week" she was saying.

Ouch! I couldn't switch off the conversation in my ear. It was too intense, as though it contained a volcano of passion, frustration and anger; all fuelled by a reservoir of desire. It was an overpowering cocktail and I was glad to be sitting facing away from her. There was something about that sultry voice that had echoes of my own childhood. Perhaps it triggered an ancient memory of a domineering relative?

Get out of it – that's someone else's life – my conscience screamed. Leave them their privacy! But the controlling voice behind me had enormous power.

"Well, I like Gary," she was saying, in a low and sexy voice. "He turns me on . . ." I could the calculation in her phrasing, keeping whoever it was on the hook. "… In his own sweet way; so I've no intention of reducing my list of friends, thank you." She paused to drink her own coffee for a moment. "Oh you did, did you – well how wrong could you be?"

I winced at this. What had the poor soul on the other end dared to say? That he thought they were an item? The crushing power of her response was surely disproportionate to her partner's plea. I wondered if I was inadvertently witnessing a long-coming explosion that had been suppressed for some time. From a few feet away, it sounded like a war of vengeance.

I sipped some of my coffee to take my mind off the perfumed assault on my senses from the rear; but the voice had begun to modify, becoming more silky, quite deadly in its sensuality, the soft and curling tones seeming to echo in the depths of my coffee mug.

"Well, I might, if you're nice to me," she chortled to the anonymous victim. "And I've never complained about your lack of imagination," she laughed out loud as her victim said something. "Don't want much, do you? But you'll have to wait, as I won't be back until next weekend."

"For heaven's sake," I muttered in a whisper, hunched forward into the dregs of my coffee; hoping my voice was beneath her hearing range. "Give me a break . . "

"What makes you think I'm doing this out of revenge?" the honeyed voice continued.

I put my hands over the back of my head, covering my ears with the heels of my palms. Stop it.

There was the sound of a chair scraping behind me. Then, the mystery person brushed past me, and a leather handbag bumped across my right shoulder, helping to ease its owner through the narrow space between the tables. There was a thumping sound as a book escaped from the bag and crashed onto my table, spinning my – thankfully nearly empty – coffee cup into a tumbling sideways motion. In panic, I reached out and tried, unsuccessfully, to stop the mug from falling. I heard her mobile phone click shut.

"Sorry," said the honey voice, "Keep the change . . ."

This was all happening in a whirl. Keep the change? Why . . .?

And then I looked up, and saw the perfumed woman in the flowing summer dress, the expensive headscarf and the large sunglasses grinning at me through the cafe windows; just before she disappeared across the road and into the promenade car park.

Gone forever . . .But there had been something in the look. Something for me, though, heaven knows I was better off far away from that chemistry . . . though I had to admire her sheer power of presence . . .

In a state of total confusion. I looked down at the book that had been dropped on my wreck of a table-top. Like the small-scale tide of coffee that had spread across the few inches either side of my upended mug, the realisation of what had just happened was seeping into my awareness.

The book was entitled "The Enneagram of Passions and Virtues" by Sandra Maitri. It was one of the very best text books on the subject and had been a well-loved friend for many years, as my own knowledge had been tested and had grown. There was a bookmark in one of the pages. I let the volume slide open at the selected chapter, grinning like an idiot in confirmation of my suspicions as the section on the Enneatype 8 came into view.

The devious, clever, manipulative . . . but what a perfect way to show understanding!

I began to chuckle at myself. My concern for Alexandra's wellbeing fell away, replaced by a new certainty. The spilled coffee, the dropped book, the overload of events; had all conspired to rob me of objectivity, as the mystery woman, in headscarf and Dolce Vita sunglasses, had disappeared across the street, swallowed up by the traffic.

Only now did it all fall into place.

The new mug of coffee being put down by Rose on the freshly tutted and wiped tabletop was a surprise, as was the bill for three lattés . . .

"She said you'd understand," chortled Rose, in her 'seen it all before,' voice. "Said you had it coming!"

She retreated to the counter, laughing. I wondered how far away the lady in the Summer dress – Alexandra – was now? She had not been late at all. She had, in fact, arrived somewhat earlier than me, and taken the seat behind where we normally spent our Monday get-togethers. Perfectly, wickedly disguised, but thankfully, not as intent on true revenge as a Type 8 could be. Now, she was on a speeding train, headed for her weekday office, in London. Marks out of ten, teacher? said the superbly acted vamp in my head; sitting back in her train seat, and taking out her legal notes . . .

Twenty Five

I knew it was Alexandra. I could feel her strong presence as she entered the cafe for our Monday morning chat. Even though I could not see it, I could tell, exactly, the moment that she stood still to take in the scene, unmoving by the doorway, gazing across the busy tables, her vision locking on to the spectacle . . .

I had worn the best of my suits. Following a purge of what turned out to be fourteen of them, I had three remaining, of which this plain blue travel suit was the best. It was freshly laundered and pressed. It felt strange to be back in it after three years of living the very opposite of the IT corporate life from which I had departed. Chinos and a good shirt were my usual 'best dressed' these days.

But she wasn't looking at the unusual sight of me in a suit . . .

Around me was a circle of silent people. Despite the usual crush of Monday morningers, as we had come to know them (and us), there was an eerie quiet over several tables on either side. They were waiting, as people often do in this situation. They were waiting to find out why the usual emotional space in which they lived had been 'stopped'.

You needed the eyes of good friends in a scene like this. Good friends need not be those you already know – in fact, they are often completely new to you; and hence of the moment, which is everything. My particular good friends of this moment of presence were a rotund couple, presumably grandparents of the two red-faced and excited children, both in stripey tops and clutching buckets and spades still in the post-purchase netting. Several minutes prior, the children had caught my conspiratorial wink, and had, gleefully, winked back at me, whispering to a silent and astonished Janet and John senior that there was a game being played . . . Children are wonderful accomplices, if you solicit their help at the right moment.

There is also, of course, the danger of a real madman, so people are cautious, too. But I wasn't radiating the same sort of vibes you would get in that situation. I was making it comic, but unexplained, and that can be a powerful combination, as mime artists throughout history would attest.

There was a cough behind me.

"It deserved a response," I said, looking at Janet and John senior but not talking to them. I winked again at the kids, who crushed together and waved their little legs in glee.

"It was that good?" Alexandra said to the back of my neck.

"It was better than that . . ."

"Will I need to help you drink your coffee?" she asked.

"No, but you might straighten my tie, if you would be so kind – I think it has twisted a bit."

"It has," she said, leaning over our usual small coffee table and adjusting the oversized, orange knot I had carefully tied an hour ago, before wresting myself into the suit jacket at the back of the car.

"The tie would be one of nine you have left, I take it?"

I laughed at the cleverness of that. "Yes, I used to have nine, but we have only one remaining."

"Nine of nine?" she asked.

"Of course!"

"Going out in style?"

"A suitable response to that magnificent performance of yours last week!"

I heard her chuckle. "Well, a girl's gotta graduate some time . . ."

"Can you turn around and drink your coffee?" she asked.

"Can't possibly," I said, rolling my eyes at Janet junior who giggled and shook her head, certain that one couldn't.

"Because the Nine has his head backwards by virtue of a jacket, shirt and tie that cover his back and not his front."

"Nope," said the reversed man. "Now, you've stopped trying and are getting piqued!"

I heard her sit down and drink some coffee. The whole cafe had dropped into silence. It can be like that, being creatively different or an idiot, depending on your perspective; but, if you stick with it, amazing things can happen.

There was an audible in-breath, the sort you'd take if you were a barrister and about to make your closing address. Then she let it out and giggled. "The suit isn't turned around – you are!"

"Big difference?" the reversed man asked.

"Huge difference." I could feel her neck straightening as the point of the charade came clear.

"He's turned away . . . he's fully equipped for the best of life if he were just to use it, but he's turned away!"

"Metanoia." I said.

"Metawhata?"

"Greek. Metanoia was wrongly translated when the versions of the Bible we use today were being assembled." I could feel her listening. "Metanoia was rendered as 'repent', but its root word means a turning around."

"'Unless ye turn around' . . ." said my clever and learned friend. "To face what?"

"To face where you came from – our shared divine origin. I looked at John junior's shining eyes and smiled back, drawing a pretend halo over my head - quite difficult in a backwards suit. He laughed with me and swung his feet again, enjoying the strangest Punch and Judy show he'd ever seen.

"I get it," she said, much closer than she should have been. With a strength I didn't know she possessed, she spun my chair around and I looked up into eyes which were shining every bit as much as John junior's. "I get it," she repeated, as I ground to a halt. "Now drink your bloody coffee and let all these people have their breakfast!"

There was spontaneous applause at her actions, as everyone returned to a normal Monday morning. But there were tears in her eyes. "But someone from 'in life' had to swing you around didn't they?" she said.

I looked back with tenderness into the tears. Shaking my head, I started to speak, "It's a mirr. . ." But she hung her head and sniffed, speaking very low; really getting it.

"It wasn't you that was turned around, was it . . . " It was not a question.

"No," I said softly. Leaning forward and planting a small kiss on the top of her head. "No."

"And you did all this for me," she looked up and around at a room returned to its normal state.

"For anyone who comes to the gate and asks," I said softly.

It was a little while later. I had, at Alexandra's insistence, put my jacket on correctly, and removed my tie. At least I now just looked like a vicar, she had said, leaving for her train.

Rose arrived at my table with a fresh coffee. She had a mischievous twinkle in her eyes. I looked down at the coffee cup. She had placed the saucer upside down on the cup's rim. On the top of the inverted saucer were a neatly folded bill and a delicately-balanced, heart-shaped chocolate from a Black Magic selection.

"Five coffees and two ice creams." she barked, smiling into my open-mouthed response. "Three for you and the lady, and the rest for your backstage team behind – it's the least you can do."

I could only agree; and turned to smile at the four happy faces grinning at me, tucking into the additional course.

"And the chocolate?"

"Made me cry, too – you idiot; and I've no idea why . . ."

Behind me, John junior's legs were swinging, happily, making the whole floor tremble.

Twenty Six

There was a chill wind as I took up my appointed place outside the doorway of our Monday morning cafe. The Summer had been a poor one for the North of England. Now, it looked as though the Autumn was about to arrive prematurely. I pulled my too-thin rain mac around my collar for warmth in the breeze blowing in from the dark sea.

It was already 08:45, fifteen minutes into our regular meeting time. Through the glass of the doorway, I could see Alexandra drinking her coffee and looking worried that I was so late. Five minutes later, she checked her phone, for the fourth time, looking for reasons for this uncharacteristic laxity on my part.

I was standing to one side of the door and could only be seen by people coming in and out. To those inside the cafe I was invisible – but, because of the refraction of the bright light, I could see, clearly, into the interior.

I watched, sad that it had to be this way, but conscious of the greater purpose of the uncharacteristic act. I watched as she finished her second coffee, then looked, one last time, at her phone, checking it for messages and then getting to her feet, reluctant to leave the space in which so many of our meaningful encounters had taken place.

She stopped in the opened doorway when she saw me, standing stock still and making no effort to enter. "You've not been there all the time . . ." her head shook in disbelief. " . . . Have you?"

I nodded. Looking deeply into those hazel eyes and holding out the small envelope I had brought. It contained a home made card.

"A little farewell present," I said.

"Farewell!" Her voice withered as the implication sank in. "Why? Have I let you down?"

"Quite the opposite," I said, smiling sadly. "You've been a wonderful pupil."

"Then why?" It was a plea, and nearly a cry.

"I have to say goodbye to what you are." I said.

"To what I am?"

"Yes," I said. "There is no other way."

"There's always a way – you showed me that!"

"Not for this . . . this is different." My tone was gentle. This was hard, and could only be approached head-on.

"Goodbye? – just like that, after all we've done; all the work and humour and all your efforts?" She clutched at the door frame to steady herself. "You've played tricks on me before – granted always with a higher purpose. Is this another?"

"No trick," I said. "I have to say goodbye to what you are . . ."

"Wait, wait," she said, pushing me further up the pavement to allow a couple into the coffee shop. "'to what I am' – that's very specific language . . ."

It was the cue I needed. I pushed the card into her hand, saying nothing. She looked down at it as though it was cursed. "Do I open it now?" She sounded dejected.

"It might make you feel better . . ."

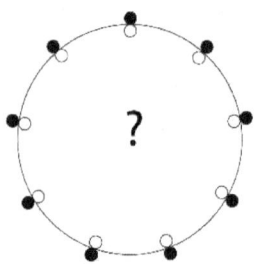

I watched as she tore open the envelope. Inside was a plain white card comprising two pages. The inner sheet, where the greeting normally is, contained a stark image of a circle with black and white dots along its perimeter line. I leaned to kiss Alexandra on the cheek and, wordlessly, strode off across the marine drive, leaving her there; mute but raging.

At that moment, I hated myself, but there was no other way . . .

What would she make of the card? Would it speak to her?

Twenty Seven

The first test would be to see whether Alexandra would be there, at all; the second would be whether she would launch a stream of invective at me, slapping down her written 'resignation' and thumping it for final punctuation in very British style.

My first latte was half cold by the time I drank it. No show … I felt sad.

I collected my things, lowering my head to pick up the battered leather folder I sometimes carried to these meetings. As my leg straightened to push me back to a standing position, the hand landed on my shoulder, spinning me around and back into the old wooden chair, which somehow managed to stay vertical, though not unmoved.

"I …"

"No!", the familiar voice said. But with an interesting overtone.

"I …" I said, attempting once again to explain how glad I was to see her.

The hand that had assaulted me flashed towards me, again, but this time with a gentler manoeuvre: she pulled up my chin with her long fingers and placed one of them over my lips, symbolically sealing them.

"Not one word," she said. "Not till I've had my say."

She sat down. In what could only have been a pre-arranged move, Rose came over with two coffees. She looked down at the delight in my eyes and returned it with a withering look that spoke of an indulgence not earned.

Alexandra took out a sealed letter from her black handbag and slapped it down in front of me.

"Open it!"

Pleased at the determination of her response, I sliced open the pristine white legal envelope with my thumb nail and spread out the single sheet of paper next to my coffee.

She had taken my image, scanned it in, and added some things. It was a clever response – exactly what I had been looking for; but, beyond that, it was a response from the heart.

"You weren't trying to get rid of me – it was a test; a kind of first level graduation?"

Playing by her rules, for now, I remained mute and nodded.

"One circle, but an inside and an outside, " she said, "For all my cleverness, I was on the outside?"

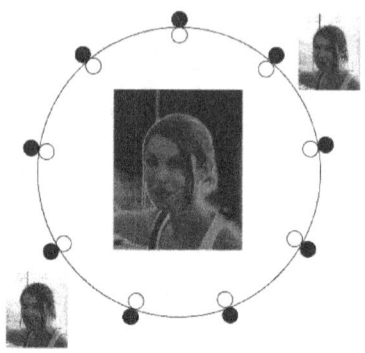

Again, I nodded.

"Good," she finally breathed out and sipped some of her coffee. "So, to be on the inside is not a matter of 'joining' some secret body; it's a state of mind and … heart."

This time I didn't need to nod; the smile said it all.

I broke my silence. "Gurdjieff called it the circle of conscious humanity; it's not that we need to 'join' anything, just to wake up to our true state and realise that the world is not what it had seemed."

"And exploring that state is the next step – my next step if I get it right?"

"Yes," I said happily. "And you have got it right … The next stage is different, but it builds on what you've already done."

"Will we still use the enneagram?" Alexandra asked.

"The enneagram is really like a compass," I said, taking my own coffee and letting the words find themselves, or as my best friends would say, getting the hell out of the way . . . "It comes into and drops out of our quest, but it's never far away. It's only a symbol; a glyph, don't forget that. The real journey is fluid and formless and takes place, as you have seen, within." I paused to let that sink in, then continued. "The real value of the enneagram is that its structure allows the incorporation of some major insights into the psyche – insights that were not easily expressible in the past; though there were those great minds who could ..."

She was silent for several minutes. Then, 'So what happens next?"

"Next, we use something different as a basis for exploration of the human spiritual journey, but we look for clues in the language of what we have already learned."

She looked wistfully at her coffee. It feels like we've come a long way ... It would all have been Greek to me a year ago!'

"Greek to me," I said. "That's interesting .... done much Greek?"

"Language?" she shook her head. "Nothing beyond the basic tourist stuff, but I always loved the myths ..."

"Which ones did you like best?"

"The Labours of Hercules. They were the most mysterious ... and the most odd."

"Would you like to revisit them and see if they contain anything of spiritual value?"

"Love too ..."

"Time for us both to do some homework, then." I added, looking at my watch. "And for you to be on your way to London."

I watched her go, glad we were still working together and smiling at her choice of subject matter. It was going to be an interesting time ... in the back of my mind the figure of Apollo was smiling.

Nine Deadly Sins

Part Two

ALEXANDRA

Twenty Eight

I was late into the coffee shop that Monday morning. My black briefcase was stuffed with information about the Greek myths that I'd printed from the internet. There was a lot on the net about the Labours of Hercules – or Heracles, to give him what I assumed to be his rightful name.

He was sitting at our usual table; two lattés in front of him, one of them half drunk, the other half cold. He smiled as I appeared in a whirlwind of apologies. "Sorry," I blurted out. "Nothing simple …"

He got the drift. "Morning Alexandra. One of those days where a series of small disasters conspire?" he said.

It was the perfect description, but I refused to go into detail. Our meetings were brief enough, without wasting time on trivial things. I looked across at his calm face. I had known him for a long time and our relationship had spanned many incarnations – from friend of the family to the present state of 'mystical teacher'; a title he had always resisted, saying that he was simply sharing a journey.

"Particularly now," he said, out of the blue, in the way he could, sometimes. "You were, perhaps thinking about the changing relationship we enjoy and our new agenda?"

I took a deep breath. Sometimes, there was about him a sense of timelessness, as though the 'now' were filled with something far bigger than he was. Not that he cut a particularly imposing figure, anyway. He was of medium height and had lost most of the hair on the top of his head. The skin on the back of his hands had started to wrinkle with age and he didn't walk with the same spring in his step that I remembered from my teens.

I supposed he was a perfectly average sixty-year old; but inside me, I hadn't wanted that; hadn't wanted him to age, since I had always looked up to the sort of person he had been to me – someone who was that bit different;

someone who would cut through the sort of trivia that the rest of the world seemed to enjoy, and describe how you were feeling in a simple word or two – as he had just demonstrated.

"The Greek Myths?" he asked quietly. "You wanted us to explore the possible deeper meanings of the Twelve Labours of Hercules?"

"Heracles," I interjected. "Hercules is an unnecessary westernised change."

"I agree," he said, easily. "Let's use Heracles, then. I can see your homework, "he pointed at my bulging briefcase. "–it looks like you've done a fair amount of research?"

I was both pleased and irritated by the mountain of information in the bag. "I have, but it's all facts; whereas I have the feeling that what you want to steer me towards is of a different order to mere facts."

He sipped his coffee and answered gently, "So tell me what's wrong with facts?"

I thought carefully before answering. There was something fundamental to the understanding of myths in what was wrong with facts. "They don't represent understanding," I said. "Something else has to happen to facts to turn them into understanding."

"Why don't we just learn understanding?" he asked. It sounded such a reasonable question.

"Can you teach understanding?" I asked.

"You tell me – can you?"

I thought about this. What was the difference between the two? Education was filled with the cramming of facts into young heads; exams were all about their regurgitation. Did that produce understanding? I thought not; understanding was about something different, something 'higher' that used a working of the facts to produce something more fluid; more powerful.

"You can transmit facts," I said, triumphantly. "You can't transit understanding – that has to be earned by an alchemy of the consciousness which uses facts as fuel ..."

He widened his eyes and smiled, "I'd say that was a very good answer." He paused and seemed to be listening to the moment, again. "So what does understanding have to do with myth?"

I was on the trail of something. We could both feel it, even if he already knew what it was. I tried to find words that would express this glimmer I had glimpsed.

"Myth is like a machine – a living machine that works with the layers of the mind associated with understanding and wisdom."

"I would agree," he said. "It's a bit like having a language that describes a language."

"I've met that in the law," I said. "There are constructs that are referred to as a meta-form whose job is to hold anything that belongs in that form."

"A bit like an equation in maths?"

"Exactly so," he said, smiling. "Though that might frighten most people!"

"Yes …" I thought back to the struggles I had endured with maths; and yet the concepts were so beautiful when you grasped them.

"But we don't need to be that rigorous with myth," he said, finishing his coffee. "We just need to ensure we speak the same language as the originators …"

"So what now?" I asked.

He looked at his watch. "So now you need to leave to catch your train."

I groaned and looked at my own watch – an expensive Cartier in black and gold. He was right. In my intensity of thought, combined with my late start, I had run out of time. I slurped the rest of my coffee – now luke warm, and picked up the heavy briefcase.

"Facts are like that," he said, looking at the overstuffed case under my arm. "It's much better to carry understanding. That way, you can deal with any fact …"

I looked down at my uncle John. Since my father had died, prematurely, in my mid-teens, he had always been there – but never before like this … we were entering a new phase of working together in this unexpected realm. I leaned over and planted a quick and cheeky kiss on the bald top of his head. "Next Monday?"

He looked up, warily, laughing at my affection, but not wanting it to be misinterpreted. "Most certainly," he said. "wouldn't miss it for the world …"

Twenty Nine

Somewhat disappointed in myself for last week's late arrival, I am here early, to give me time to chat to Rose. That darling lady, who runs the tea room, has watched and supported our craziness for some time.

Craziness? I don't really think so ... though, when I get off that train in London each Monday, and stiffen back into my world – what I now think of, in a dramatic reversal of attitude, as my other world – I feel I'm entering the real craziness; and that this gentle, if often dramatic probing of life and truth is the reality ...

I've changed in all sorts of ways, some of which I haven't told John about. I want him to notice, and I'm sure he does, but, I've toned down my formal dress and made plainer most of my accessories. In this there is a slight emulation of his simplicity – though I know that, in his former business world, he would have shared the crisp uniforms of indulgent excess ... He's never asked me to do this, but it's a kind of respect for the transition he must have gone through when he walked away to do 'his thing' as he often puts, it; smiling mischievously at me.

Looking at the time, I finish my friendly conversation with Rose and pick up our coffees from the counter. I refuse her kindly offer of help, and take them to the small table in the sea-facing corner – the place of our meetings. He arrives as I put down the steaming mugs.

"Morning Alexandra," he says, softly. Giving me a peck on the cheek.

"Morning John." My smile is a beam. Life is good.

He launches straight in, "Hercules–Heracles, we decided, didn't we? How are you getting on with him?"

I consider my response carefully. I've been doing my homework and it's thrown up more questions than answers. "Twelve ..." I let it hang in the air. I know it's important.

"Ah yes," he says, not mockingly. "Twelve – a fascinating number ... four times three, and three times four." He sips his coffee, watching me; and then, when I say nothing, he does one of his time-stopping things: he picks up three small packets of sugar from the bowl in the middle of the table, tears the heads off two of them in an exaggerated gesture, and smooths out the deliberately spilled contents across the inset glass top of our small, round table. The remaining packet he keeps in his left hand as he sips his coffee.

I can't see her, but I know that, behind me, Rose is planning his slow death...

"Show me twelve ..." he says, flickering his eyes at me, snake-like. For a second, I wonder how many other nieces in the world are treated like this? I stare at the surface of white sugar. What does he want? Do I write the numerals 12 in the crystals? No, he wants something deeper than that. I hold my chin in my hands, staring the sugar, while doing my best to empty my mind, letting the moment speak; enabling something that is already there to reveal itself ... within that calmed now, it does, and with a smile, I draw a near-perfect circle in the white sugar.

I look up and he nods. "How many now?"

"Not twelve ..." I'm teasing him; and enjoying it. "But it could be twelve – or as many as you want there to be ... the circle is infinitely pliable, after all."

"Good answer," he says, nodding down at the sugar. "A cycle of perfection and completeness, then, no matter how big its circumference?"

"Like the year – having twelve months and then beginning again ..."

"With the four seasons?" he asks, reasonably.

Something tells me to draw an equal-armed cross in the circle. I do so, dividing it into four quadrants. "Spring, summer, autumn, winter ..." I say.

John leans forward to hover his hand anti-clockwise over the newly quartered circle. "And who else might work here?" he asks.

I look down at the symbol I have drawn. I imagine it divided into the full twelve, with the quadrants superimposed as they are. Something pulls me to the answer.

"Why ... astrologers, I suppose? They share the use of a seasonal circle, don't they?"

"They do indeed," he replies, then adds. "In a greater and a lesser sense,"

"Greater and lesser?"

"The twelve periods of the year, which we know as the signs of the zodiac; and the long ages of the evolution of life on Earth, which is known as the precession of the equinoxes, which takes twenty-six thousand years to transit the whole zodiac and just over two thousand years to transit each of the signs."

"The Dawning of the Age of Aquarius ..." I hear myself saying, smiling at a memory of a song from my uncle's own youth that he used to sing to me as a child.

"Indeed," he says, also smiling, "Though, in truth and mathematics, it has yet to dawn."

"We're still in the great age of Capricorn?" I ask, keen to show off my pub quiz sequence of the signs.

"Almost ..." he fights a kindly smile. "Remember that the greater cycle goes backwards, so, if Aquarius is next, then we are in the age of ...?"

"Oh, I see – so that would be Pisces?"

"Yes."

"The age of the fish," I add, grasping at some of the deeper pub facts.

"And the fish was one of the key symbols of?"

Suddenly it hits, me ... This is not just an intellectual exercise. What he's starting to describe is the happening of events on a vast scale, something like the wave that we discussed so long ago, that provides great energy and superhuman challenges ... and the effects are repeated, at smaller and smaller scales as the same laws empower and challenge the evolution of more and more detailed forms of consciousness.

I cannot help saying the word he's expecting, "Christ ..."

"Christ, a figure that some would call The Saviour of the Age ... an age that is now coming to an end."

I think of a single vast circle, containing within it many other circles which share the same sectors – the same seasons of energy and challenge as deeper evolution is urged forward. I think of all the circles centred on the same point in the middle, of a rippling outwards to form the 'space' within which it all happens, and then a return home to the centre, each circle playing its essential part, each circle as important as any of the others, despite its apparent 'smallness'. He watches, perfectly still ...

"So you lead with twelve ... and Heracles?" He lets the silence be the question. Into that perfect space comes the sentiment for which I've been fishing.

"So the twelve labours are the generic – the cosmically derived – labours we must all face on the way to a higher level of consciousness?"

His reply is tinged with humility, "It is my belief that they were constructed that way ... but the only way to test that is to bring them to life – your life ..."

I sit back to think, and finish my coffee. While I am doing this, he leans slightly forward and asks, "What did Hercules do to deserve his labours?"

There are many answers, depending on the bias of the historian involved, but they all agree on one thing.

"He killed people close to him ..."

He leans closer, and whispers, "In one very wise version, he killed his teachers ..." He lets it hang in the air.

"Killed his teachers?" I sit there, mute. The thought of killing one's teacher is appalling ... and then I see, between the stark words, that there is another meaning to this. I want to share it with him, but he's stood up and gone to fetch a pan, brush and wiping cloth from Rose, who is grinning at the counter, pleased at his seeming contrition.

When he comes back, I'm ready. In his hand, alongside the cleaning tools, is the remaining bag of sugar. I take it from him and look deeply into his kind eyes.

"Independence," I say. "My journey and only mine ..."

Matching his earlier violence, I rip the head off the sugar and pour it onto the drawn circle, scattering my symbolic atoms into the space of creation, freeing them from all conditioning patterns.

He says nothing, just bends to plant a kiss on the top of my head, then hands me the pan and brush.

"Your first labour, then ..."

Thirty

Over the weekend, one image from the Heracles myth had haunted me – that of the victorious hero wearing the lion skin – particularly the head. The picture of the two heads occupying the same space remained in my mind right up to the moment that I entered our cafe on the Monday morning.

John was there when I arrived; but he was sitting with his back to me, at our usual table, in what was normally my chair. Rose, the owner, nodded to me as I entered the cafe, following my gaze and looking warily at my uncle, as though wondering what madness he was to perform this week.

I advanced on the figure. "That's my chair," I said.

"How do you know?" the back said.

I thought about that carefully, looking over his shoulder at the two coffees. Like a sentry to pleasure he barred my way, but without violence.

"Are you going to stand there, forever?" he asked.

"Are you ever going to turn around?" I responded, in retaliation.

"But I'm facing you!"

I couldn't help but burst out laughing. "No you're not," I chortled. "You're facing nothing ..."

"A harsh way to describe an empty chair ..." he said. "Come and fill it."

Something still barred my way – something in me. What was this? What essence of the now lay in this curious arrangement that was becoming more serious by the second, whispering look, look deeper, as I stood there, mute to his request.

"Turn around!" I said, unable to bear the tension any more.

"When you sit opposite me I shall be turned around," he said, softly.

I heard myself shout, "No you won't ..." And then, in a burst of energy that was part anger and part emotional release, I reached to shake his chair, forcing him to stand and, now grinning, turn to face me – but backing into his usual place as he did so. The effect was surreal. He sat down without speaking, still smiling at me. There was no threat at all, and yet my hair felt like it was standing on end …

"It's empty," he said, gesturing to my seat, which had grown in importance to the point of being explosive. "But it's not the same, is it?"

I sat down, clumsily; disliking this assault on my normality. My face had reddened and I must have appeared confused. I looked around, certain that everyone would be staring at me. As I scanned table after table, I could see that no-one was … except Rose, who held my gaze with an intense power and a deep smile which seemed to urge me on.

None of this was making any sense … and my heart was racing.

"Who are you, now?" he asked me, with nothing but warmth in his expression.

"Who …wha?" I whispered.

"Heracles and his labours …" John said, switching the topic as though he'd just finished chewing a biscuit. "At what point do you think they begin?" He was still moving backwards; becoming smaller as other things pressed into my now.

My lips were moving without words. My mind racing with images of court cases where I had been forced to reach deep into my mental and emotional reserves. One in particular loomed large in memory: a crook – a fraudster – trying to convince the jury that he had not wronged an honest man. His barrister had been so slick, so very clever, and they were winning the case …

"Both chairs were always there …" John's voice in the background was saying. Be quiet, be quiet. My wordless lips framed the injunction, as the man on the witness stand looked across with confidence at his adviser, and I fixed him with eyes grown full with confidence … because I had seen the falseness of what he was saying; had seen the small hole in the armour they had welded him into …

"Their two-ness is necessary, but only one of them can drive the twin self," the distant voice droned on. "And when that happens with intent, then the man …"

I was losing it. Things were rushing down a long tube, the end of which was bright – very bright. I opened my mouth to speak and the defendant opened his, forming the same words on his lying lips; his barrister rising to his feet in alarm at the turn of events; at the way the puppet had switched owners …

"Then the man can act from within …" the distant voice said.

The lying defendant spoke the truth, the vital word coming from his mouth, with his barrister screaming behind me and the judge banging his gavel to restore order …

"Then the man can act from within the lion's mouth, because the man, who was never just a man, can reveal that he was always …"

"The sole responsible party," said the defendant.

"The solar force," said the man within the lion's head.

"The soul," said my lips; not to a cafe full of disinterested people, but to the far-away relative opposite, who was suddenly closer – so close that I could feel the warmth of his smile; and that of Rose who had come to stand behind me.

Soon after, I was gazing out at the sea. No-one was speaking. My coffee remained untouched. Instead, Rose had brought me a cup of tea, saying, "Hot sweet tea – can't beat it after a shock like that, love."

John's voice was almost subvocal, "And so Heracles begins his labours at the point where he sees that he is …?"

"A soul incarnated in a necessary but devious body, rather than a body aspiring to be a soul …" I said, watching the judge leave the courtroom, shaking his head in amusement; and the guilty man's barrister slamming his brief case onto the bench.

But the guilty man looked peaceful … more peaceful than I had ever seen him, before.

Thirty One

 The last time I was in here, I had glimpsed something. Insight had flickered and shifted as the concentrated presence of John and, surprisingly, Rose, had nudged me none-too-gently towards my moment of 'seeing'. Now, I wanted to know more …

"It's about where you put the "I", isn't it?" I asked John, as he sat down, late with latté, and smiled, apologetically, at me.

"Where is the 'I' now?" he asked, smiling over the hot coffee he was trying to sip, to catch up with mine.

"That's what I'm wrestling with," I responded, trying not to lose the thread that I had carefully assembled in the past week, parts of which were trying to sneak away in the face of the lovable but infuriating man who might just help me unravel it.

I fought to remember the moment of revelation, wanting to replay it. "If the real adventures of Heracles begin when the adventurer realises that they are soul in body, then that shift is one of perspective," I paused to sip my own coffee. "And that shift empowers something within us to start acting in a different way?"

"Or something else to just to get out of the way," he said, flatly.

"Out of the way?"

I watched him dig deep, "Or empowers what we think of as 'us' to get the hell out of there and let something more authentic have its say … or maybe just its 'look'."

This was all moving too quickly. I pondered the idea of 'it's look'. "Wouldn't that have always been there?" I asked; reasonably I thought.

"So what changed in that moment," he probed, leaving me to grapple with the subtlety of this razor's edge.

I thought long and hard before responding, "The power of the 'I's' position changed" I said. "Moving inward, it moved beyond the limitations of the ordinary world, revealed, with its new vision, as the limited sphere it always was.

"And what else did it move beyond?" John asked, fixing me with that look, again.

Something surged; an excitement, a rushing sense. I knew the answer.

"Reaction!" I exclaimed. "The location of the sense of 'I' moved beyond the place of reaction ... and felt empowered because it was somewhere more real!"

"So 'more real' simply reveals a better, a truer, perspective, whose power ...?" He left it dangling. I was working for my coffee, even though I had bought them. Within the silk blouse, I could feel my skin glistening with the effort of concentration.

"Whose power ..." I replied, grasping the torch. "Is the removal of illusion ..."

"And how did we draw habitual illusion," he pressed me, leaning closer. My heart was racing. I wondered if Rose had come to stand behind me, again. Draw it? What could he mean.

Before my eyes, he was flicking his fingers up, one by one, from his coiled fists. He stopped with the second thumb unused.

"The enneagram?" I asked, incredulous. "The enneagram is about the removal of illusion?"

"I did call it a truth machine," he said, fully opening both hands in a gesture that reminded me of wings unfurling. "So we know the nine-fold nature of what has to be removed," he paused to take a long drink of coffee, choosing his words, carefully. "Or, rather, refined – since much of it will be needed for the new 'seer' to be effective in the world – much like the triumphs of Heracles ..."

I sat back, conscious of the time, and wanting to use my last Monday moments to harvest the right insights to take away for the week.

"So the Heracles stories are a special kind of adventure?" I asked, draining the coffee before continuing. "One that would have an effect beyond the normal way of learning in the world?"

He smiled in a way that beamed warmth. "One might say that they would attract the disciples of learning."

The moment was complete. The bombshell to be taken away, uncommented on. We both knew it; no further words were needed. A new and often silent language of interaction was developing between us.

I hefted my black bags onto the chair, and then, still wordless, I leaned over to kiss the old curmudgeon on the cheek. I could feel him chuckling at my departing back as I opened the venerable, art deco glass door and re-entered the world beyond our cafe.

Thirty Two

"They have a new menu," he said casually.

I felt myself tense; then got hold of it, recognising the reaction and how it had absorbed me into the moment in a bad way: making me identify with the building anger, rather than watching it unfold as a thing in its own right ... losing me, in other words; losing me, that all-important sense of being present, rather than being mechanical. He had, I had to admit, taught me certain things well ... so why, this Monday morning, did I have a mounting sense of 'smug git' as I looked at him?

John held up the computer-printed coffee menu. "It says they have recognised that their clientele fall into three bands." He spoke evenly, in measured tones. There was no hint of his overbearing side; which was why I was suspicious ... "It says that they are going to offer three levels of coffee from now on: 'Good and Basic', by which I take it to mean that old fashioned black or white coffee with no Italian frills," he paused to look at me over his reading glasses, nodding when I appeared attentive. "'A Continental Range', by which I assume they mean Italian-derived staples, such as cappuccino and latté ..." he sipped his own latté, looking slightly peeved that he'd only achieved mid-range on the new scale. "... and 'Something Special' which includes extra flavourings like vanilla and flashes of genius like a chai tea latté." He put down the folded paper, looking across at me for a verdict. I sipped my own coffee and said nothing ... The phrase 'smug git' was still writing itself on the surface of my wresting consciousness. I had first called him it on my sixteenth birthday; having learned it from a friend on whom I was, at that time, modelling myself. He had made some closing point in an argument. It was an unassailable piece of logic and I had wanted to bring him down a peg or two, so I said it to his face ...

It was the first time I had been conscious of psychologically hurting an adult.

It was also the first time I had watched someone else wrestle with themselves, not externally, for he kept his cool admirably, as uncles are supposed to do; but inside, where the barb had struck and stuck. Looking back on that moment I realised that he had known that he could, indeed, be a 'smug git', and had probably tried, without too much success, to suppress it. Five minutes after I had said it, it was forgotten, and the dinner party picked up without damage. He had, over the years, reminded me of it, but never with rancour ... always with a joke, a remembering of a shared gateway to a different world – for us both.

"A bit like the myths, then?" he said, softly, across from me now, in a voice that was very different to then.

"Like the myths ... coffee?" I asked.

"The three levels of meaning," he said simply.

My head was starting to whirl. From unwarranted annoyance, to long-ago memories, to coffee and ... myths? "You've lost me!" I said, taking a deep breath and trying hard to direct my attention to what he was saying.

"The best of the myths, from whenever they derive, often have three levels of meaning."

I sat up, concentrating as I would in a legal situation. "Give me an example," I said.

"We'll come to the Greeks, later," he said, "But let's take a classic – the different ways to describe the truth in the Gospels.

I pretended to look shocked. "You're taking the Gospels as myth!"

"In the best way possible, yes ..." he responded, but that' s for another day ... what I wanted to do was to take situations you would recognise to illustrate a point."

"Okay," I said, playing it cool.

"How did they represent truth in the Old Testament?" he asked me.

I wracked my brains; religion had never done much for me, despite John's attempts to get me to see 'under the covers' as he had often said. From somewhere, the image of Moses surfaced, standing, in the pages of my childhood's illustrated Bible, on a mountain, holding up huge tablet of ...

"Stone ..." I said, triumphantly.

"Exactly!" he enthused. "Stone ... Tell me the properties of 'stone'."

I was onto this, now. I could see that this was an interesting avenue of exploration.

"Fixed," I said. "As in 'set in stone'."

"Exactly. So the older concept of truth would be something that is still with us: the letter of the law …"

I cringed at that. How often had I railed at the legal system that made all of us who earned our living under its wings reduce our thoughts to the most simple forms of logic. And how unfair some of the results of that were.

"We should be able to do better, in this day and age, but how could we measure it?"

"Another day," he said. "Or you'll miss your train." He rotated the forefinger of his right hand. "Now fast forward to the Gospels. How was Jesus baptised into the truth of what was to be a short, dramatic and painful ministry?"

The ideas were flowing … I could feel as well as see where this was headed. "With water," I said, watching the words fly through the space to his gently knowing face.

"And water is …?"

"Not stone," I answered, entering the mystery he had set. "Not stone at all. It flows around things, it's all connected …" I pulled my head up as a revelation hit home. "It's whole!"

John was nodding. "Whole, indeed," he said. "So the Gospels moved the concepts of truth on, but did they stop at water?"

Now I was struggling. I wracked my brains but couldn't think. John looked at his watch and shook his head. It was an easy gesture; with no impatience. "No matter," he said. "and next week, we'll finally begin to look at one of the Labours of Heracles – armed with a certain knowledge that truths are represented in different ways and on different levels, depending on who they're addressed to." He paused to finish his coffee. "But, for now, I must go. He tapped his jaw, wincing slightly. "Dentist. Need a filling, I think …"

Just before leaving he pushed the new drinks menu across the table to me. "Interesting reading," he said.

As the old glass door swung shut I looked at my watch and realised that he had left early. I had time to finish my own coffee and peruse the new delights being offered by Rose's establishment. Not bothering with the cover, I went straight for the detail. Sure enough, there were the three categories of hot drinks, labelled: Good and Basic; Continental; and Something Special.

And then my eyes saw it. Right at the bottom of the page was a single paragraph: 'For those of us of sufficient years who have developed their ability to taste, we offer a small selection of fine wines.'

And then I noticed that there were no prices against any of the items on the menu. Beginning to smile, I turned the unread front cover into view. There, in simple block letters were the words:

The Smug Git Cafe
presents:
The Truth of the Matter

;<)

I was still smiling as I swung my black bags onto the carriage and climbed aboard my week.

Thirty Three

"I've had a week of threes," I said, wanting to seize the initiative. I felt empowered, full of energy; and I wanted to be at it ... the labours of Heracles, that is.

He looked at me over a succession of objects: the coffee cup, poised next to his bemused lips; the newspaper, held in his free hand until I arrived and tapped its top; and the reading glasses sitting halfway down his nose. "Good morning," he replied, beaming; then, chuckling to himself, he added, "Threes? Tell me about the threes."

I calmed myself down, digging deep for the essence of what I wanted to say. "Each group of three has a purpose, a possibility of growth from one to two to three. Getting to three would be the end of that cycle ... for the small ones."

"There are big ones, too?" he asked.

"Yes – there are very big ones, overarching stages, in which the smaller sets of three are building blocks."

"And you feel you might be making a transition between two of these very big ones?" He smiled. It was a kindly smile, full of encouragement.

"A kind of jumping between levels," I responded, desperate to find that right word. "A fundamental change of direction... a moment of 'no going back'."

"Ah ..." he said, sipping his coffee. "An initiation ..."

I sat and drank my own. Initiation. It was a word I had heard many times. It conjured up bad horror films or scary fiction. Was there a different side to it? Had I stumbled with my earnest words upon something that was really rather special ... and personal? Was there a world of real initiation where those involved wouldn't dream of demeaning it in fiction?

"It's a deeply personal thing," John said, reading the thoughts in my mind. "Initiation can only belong to the person going through it. Other people can help with the environment that assists it, but the gateway to that 'fundamental change', as you so rightly called it, admits only one passenger."

I was fighting to stay level with his concepts; as often happened; yet I knew how far I had come in understanding in the past year; I could feel it, taste it and, sometimes, in a moments of extreme clarity, see it.

"So tell me," I said without sarcasm. "What this has to do with the Labours of Heracles?"

John sat back, closing his eyes in a way that I hadn't seen before. He sipped his sightless coffee and waited. I knew that his introspection had nothing to do with making me wait.

At last he spoke, "What you are experiencing is the start of initiation, which is truly wonderful, given that you've had so little instruction …"

He closed his eyes again, this time for longer. I waited, practically breathless, until he surfaced.

"I've been trying not to use ancient words," He sipped his coffee through a wry smile. "But sometimes they are too good not to use." His eyes flicked up from the coffee cup to look at me. There was calmness and clarity in them, as they brought something very special into the moment.

"You, along with Heracles, are being initiated into the world of the disciple."

The eyes didn't leave me, measuring my inner and outer reactions to this shock of a statement. "Disciple?" I muttered, quite flummoxed by the notion. "Like the disciples of Jesus you mean!"

"The word and the concept are older than the story of Christ," he said, softly. "And don't be put off by the gravity of the Gospel stories; no-one is expecting you to sell all your possessions and follow some wandering Teacher."

"Not even you, then?" I regretted the words as soon as I had uttered them. I closed my eyes in a gesture of apology, shaking my head. "I didn't–"

"I know," he said. "It's okay. We all do irrational things when the ego is threatened by some profound truth. In this case the profound truth belongs to you, alone, and is to do with an inner realisation you have already had. It has nothing to do with me as your so-called 'teacher'." He fell silent, but added a few seconds later, "But, in any event, you would not be my disciple – I don't have any; that destiny is reserved for others of much more importance …"

Before I could speak, he added, "In any case, your greatest teacher is the one who is calling you … your own Soul."

It took me a while to speak. "So, everything I'm feeling ... sensing ... is part of a call to a different journey?"

"Yes," he said. "It's a call to those who begin to see the world differently – very differently; to those who realise that we could practically rip up most of what we were taught, because the world – the real world beyond received illusion – is a ball of singing life much richer and infinitely more beautiful that the outer layer that science does its honest best to describe ..."

"And what does that journey entail?" I asked, my voice a whisper.

"Going backwards," he laughed, rocking with the mirth of an inner meaning that he knew I could not yet fathom. He coughed, apologetically, then continued, "The new journey imposes the Will of the inner you on the world you react to; and thereby tests and cleanses it ..."

"It will test and cleanse me?"

"Only those parts of you that need it," he said, the eyes never leaving mine. "It knows; trust me, it knows ..."

"The journey is intelligent?" I gasped at the thought, watching him nod at me, seeing the fullness of the meaning take root in my mind and heart.

"So now to the Labours," he smiled, brushing aside my disbelief. "And so you must study the nature of wild female horses."

"Not lions?" I asked, surprised that my preparation had been tripped up.

"No," he answered. "We are to follow Heracles around the Zodiac, anticlockwise – the world of the changed direction, beginning with the Wild Mares of Aires, in the symbolic Spring."

He tapped his watch, wordlessly. As he got up to go, he bent to whisper, "Lovely new coat."

The unseasonably warm October weather had continued. "I don't have a coat on," I protested, still stunned by the whole encounter.

"Minerva has given you a robe," he said. "though few will see it ..." Then, he kissed me on the top of my head. "We are allowed to be proud of our children."

Thirty Four

"Wild horses," I said, sitting down with both our coffees and passing his across our small table.

"Wild women horses!" John replied, a glint in his eyes.

"Okay, then, wild women horses, if you must. But you said we were now, in our studies, in Aries, the sign of the ram, surely?" I watched him nod. "So why wild horses?"

"I do not have definitive answers to some of these," he said. "I often have to go away and study them, too." He sipped some of his hot coffee, a long-standing veteran of coffee-gone-cold in the intensity of some of our encounters. I waited … "I suspect that rams and horses were both carriers of important things, and therefore somewhat interchangeable."

"I think I can add something to that," I said, proudly. "Neptune gifted Heracles horses so that his emotions could take him farther than his thoughts, and …" I halted, for the sheer theatre of it. "… the waves of the sea are said to resemble galloping horses."

Eventually, he spoke, again, "So, lady horses – mares to be precise; let's just play with it. What do we associate with the female nature, in terms of general capabilities?"

I thought carefully, eager to be leading some of these discussions. John had indicated that, in his mind at least, I had passed some key stage, to which he had referred in our prior meeting as, 'discipleship', though the implications of that concept still concerned me.

"Knowing, now, a little of the language of myth, I would imagine that we are looking at women as exemplars of emotion."

"I would say that's absolutely right." He looked pleased. "So what happens in the story for which we can make that fit?"

I gathered my thoughts and sipped my coffee. I wanted to be as exact as possible. "Heracles is fresh into his challenge. The classic freshness and expansiveness of the natural new year – April, the spring – are therefore central to his actions. He rushes into his first task, raw and cocky, and makes a mess of it ..."

"Makes a mess?" John raised an eyebrow. "But he rounded up the Mares and saved his home region!"

"Yes, but it cost him the life of a close friend, Abderis."

"Whose relationship to Heracles was ...?"

"We don't know," I said, now not so sure.

"Yes we do," said John. "He was his inferior, someone he treated as beneath him and who he therefore left to finish the job... which he couldn't, and lost his life, accordingly"

"Okay," I said, grasping the horns, again. "So, much of this story is about levels."

"I agree," John said, cunningly. "Levels of what?"

It was there before, me, spinning and waiting to be grasped. I could feel it. I had been right in my alignment of emotions and wild horses, but they weren't just horses – the wildness was more due to where they came from. Suddenly, I had the key.

"The higher and lower selves," I shouted, causing several of the people near to us to turn and study my outburst. "Heracles is striving to act from his higher self. The mares represent untamed thoughts. They emanate from the disciple in the time of Aries because Aries rules the head, as in 'hot-headed'."

John was smiling now. "Yes," he said. "Aries is said to rule the whole of the head, very much as in 'hot-headed'; which would be a lower level of its possible function. But what of the poor man who was trampled to death?"

Like Heracles in the Aries spring, I was full of energy and passion. Nothing was going to stop me getting this right. "Hercules acted with the blind passion of the new quest, full of energy but badly directed. He delegated the all-important ending of his task to his lesser, who was killed as a result of Heracles' carelessness."

John leaned forward to finish his coffee, looking at his watch. "But Heracles did finish his task?"

I started speaking from somewhere within me. The words came tumbling out.

"But lived in despair of what his actions had cost his friend, his lower self, his personality." I could feel the hero's sadness. "But sometimes such sadness makes us very much wiser ... and the Gods smile on those who can grow in sadness."

John was standing and tapping the side of his jaw again. "Second part of the crown," he winced. Wish I'd looked after them better, particularly that one." He paused and gave me the kindest look. "So, when you engage the energy of the spring, at the start of your quest, make sure your thoughts – the mares – are well controlled and pointed in the right direction ... in other words, don't underestimate the powers of discrimination that you've spent a lifetime learning!"

The right direction? As he left I continued to wrestle with that one. How could this 'energy of the spring' have two directions?

Thirty Five

I had done my homework the previous weekend and arrived at our cafe early, eager to organise my thoughts before John arrived for our Monday get-together.

"Dark out there," he said, entering behind me and kissing the top of my head in his customary fashion before sitting down. I looked out of the window at the clear blue morning sky. We were having the most amazing autumn, though the summer had been standard issue, British wretched. I shook my head and turned back to look at him, forming the words as I finished the head-turn, only to be struck dumb by what greeted me.

"What is that?" I shrieked, trying hard not to laugh out loud and ruin the peace of Rose's morning.

"What?" he asked, innocently.

"That bright thing on your head." I responded, "And don't tell me it's dark out there–despite being late October, it could be a summer's morning!"

But it was too late; I collapsed into a mess of giggles at my idiot uncle sitting opposite me, wearing a lighted head torch and a big grin.

"Desperate to find something that worked," he glanced apologetically upwards, rolling his eyes. "Best I could do!"

I recovered some self-control. Strangely, the whole of the cafe's inhabitants were not studying the Monday lunatics, just a few of them.

"It's quite good, though," I said. "You are Mr Cyclops, I take it?"

"Ah yes…" he smiled. "And on that basis, it is double dark out there…"

I sat back, sipping my coffee, thoughtfully; just studying him. He was seldom single dimensional and some of his best teaching had, at first, seemed ludicrous.

"So, we're not on Crete, presumably because we've already been there, but we are in the month of Taurus?"

"Not on the island of Crete to be precise." he said, slightly narrowing his eyes. "And, yes, we are in the sign of Taurus, and rippling with the energy of beginnings from our trip to the Mares of Aries."

I chewed on that, taking another sip of the still-scalding coffee. "Island? Okay then," I said. "So being off the island is a good thing, though it was Crete where Heracles successfully tracked down the Bull with the shiny star on its head, helping him ride it out of the maze and across the ocean to the mainland?"

"That's very good," John said. "you should carry on…"

"So Heracles had to go somewhere…" I paused, trying to dig for the meaning I had sensed. "Separated!" I blurted into my coffee, nearly spraying the hot liquid off the surface of my cup.

His eyes did that flickery thing. He leaned forward, pushing the moment at me. "Yes," he said, enthusiastically. "Heracles had to go to Crete to gain a deep understanding of something that it is essential to know the whole of."

I sat back and drank some more coffee, catching Rose walking past and asking her for another, as I was going to run low with all this frantic thinking. John refused my offer of a second. I took a deep breath and waded in. "So, something, presumably connected with Taurus, had to be learned in finding the Bull and riding it – that's it – riding it!" I was onto the trail now, I could feel it, and see it in his gleeful eyes.

"What happens when we ride something?" he asked, innocently.

"We master it!" It was a crude description, but it would have to suffice.

"Do we kill it?"

"No," I replied, "We get the best out of it."

"So a bull could do a range of things, from pulling a plough to keeping a herd of cows happy?"

Suddenly, it was there before me. "Sex – Taurus, Venus!" I said, laughing. "Heracles went to Crete to learn to master his sexual forces, not suppressing them, but riding them back to higher beings – The Cyclopses." I had no idea what the plural was and had to improvise.

"And what relationship did the three 'Cyclopses' have to him?"

I was struggling. Barely able to suppress his mirth, he reached up and switched his single light on and off, again.

113

"He, he…" I was practically screaming inside. I knew the answer was literally shining in … in my face.

"He was one…" I whispered. "Having mastered something utterly fundamental to everything, he was able to be accepted in the company of his kind … or at least, of those he could now recognise as his kind."

"And the single light – sorry eye – in the head of the 'Cyclopses'?" John asked, pressing me while the virile energy of the Spring roared inside my laughing mind.

My voice, when it came, was dreamy. Like I was listening to someone else speak. "Single rather than dual," I said, "Seeing the higher, causal plane as the more real; seeing that there is a single light – the light of understanding that, alone, illuminates the universe; or, possibly, seeing from a unified Self…"

I stopped, timeless and, finally, wordless, staring at the stars in the constellation of Taurus.

"I think that's plenty enough for now," he said, gently. "Well done, you…"

I did not hear him get up; did not see Rose change my un-drunk coffee for a fresh one; did not hear him leave. I didn't even know, until I saw myself reflected in the cafe's window, that he had put the head torch on me, and left it switched on …

Thirty Six

I made a special effort to be at Rose's coffee shop early the next Monday morning. Despite that, he was there before me …

"Morning, John," I muttered, trying not to let my irritation show…

"Morning, Alexandra," said my uncle, cheerfully. It was only then that I noticed two things were–well, wrong… To start with he was sitting with his hands on his head, but with the palms facing upwards… he never did that. The second wrong thing was that he'd gathered every menu from the tables not in use and had stood them all upright on ours. Now that I was sitting down, I could barely see him over the vertical mass of laminated plastic.

"That's a mess," I said frankly, watching him pull that smug face. Once you were trapped in his visual logic, there was seldom an escape…

"The story of Heracles and the Golden Apples is a mess?" he asked, feigning innocence.

"No, I didn't mean–" and then I saw the gentle nudge the 'mess' was giving us–a head start on the complex myth which, at first reading, was, indeed a mess…

"Oh, yes…" I said. "That's very good…"

Rose arrived with the two lattés. I thanked her and watched her shoot a sneering glance at her long-time adversary, pretending to ignore his Manhattan skyline of a table.

"I'll put them back… promise!" he called to her departing and disgusted back.

"Drink your coffee," I urged, in mitigation of my earlier presumption.

"Can't…" he said.

"Why not?"

"Because the world will fall down…"

I stared at him, getting it quickly, this time. "Okay Atlas," I said. "Pass it to me."

"It's not a football," he responded. "You have to take it–it's a world!"

"Whose world?"

"Well, if you must know–yours! Now are you going to relieve me of it?"

Stifling a belly laugh, I got up and pretended to take the 'world' from his upturned palms, ignoring the Monday morning ridicule from the occupied tables around us – I had, at least, learned to endure that...

"You can't hold it like that," he said, grinning at me. You have to hold it over your head."

"But then I won't be able to drink my coffee!" I protested.

"But, it's your world... and you did offer!"

I fought back the urge to scream. Before me, my delicious coffee, made by the fair Italian (despite her very English name) hand of one of the finest coffee alchemists I knew, was going cold. My heart began to hammer as I realised he was serious.

"You want me to sit here like an idiot carrying nothing?"

"Like now," he asked slyly. "You sure that's nothing...?"

I could feel little beads of sweat forming on my forehead as I strained against this fate – it was so cruel...

"Prometheus thought so, too, but he endured... for others," he said, reading my mind.

In disbelief, I felt my arms rising to meet this outrageous obligation. As I did so he smiled and reached into the infamous black bag which I now noticed lying on his knee. He took something out but concealed whatever it was in his palm. He watched me suffering... I fought the hatred.

Then something happened that shook me. Rose appeared from behind our table and picked up my coffee cup, letting me sip it, gently, while she held it at an angle. She remained alongside me, emotionally sharing my fate and daring others to intervene.

John picked up the black bag and zipped it up. He smiled and came to stand next to Rose, placing on my saucer three small, gold-wrapped, chocolates. "Ferrero Rocher – closest I could find to a golden apple," he said, gently. "Well done, you..."

And then he reached for the world on my head. "I'll take this now," he said, slinging his now empty bag over his arm and carrying the world out on his head.

As he opened the cafe door with a swiftly juggled hand, I called to him, "But you've not touched your coffee!"

"Offering to the Gods..." he said, his voice fading into the drizzle of a November morning.

Rose put my coffee down in front of me. "I'll get you a fresh one on the house, to go with the Golden Apples," she said, patting my shoulder and making me cry at the kindness of others, and its ability to go where we, alone, cannot...

I felt as though there were two of me sitting, snivelling at that table–and I didn't give a damn who was watching us both.

Thirty Seven

"The story of Heracles and the Golden Apples begins with failure…" I said.

"It does," replied John, sipping his latté. "Just as, in the first story, with the Wild Mares, Heracles gets a bitter lesson that never leaves him, with his failure to protect the life of young Abderis, despite his success in overcoming the wild she-horses."

He stopped, then, and looked at me very seriously. "Failure is very important… it not only teaches us about success, it teaches us about the fragility of both – and the existence of a third … thing."

He had lowered his voice when speaking the word 'thing', as though its impact had been pivotal in his own life. For a short while I watched him drink his coffee, saying nothing. I decided we could afford to come back to it – he had, inadvertently, touched on something far below his confident exterior and I wanted to know more…

"If we didn't have adversity, we could never really do anything, could we?" I ventured.

John looked up, shocked. "That's really good," he nodded. "It touches on the basic polarity of the universe. We can only 'do' when there is a raw material to do with."

"And that is opposition?"

"Perhaps a better word is resistance, which removes the idea of hostility – though hostility may still apply…"

"So, sometimes we overcome the resistance and a new thing, a third thing, you called it, is born."

"Born, yes–excellent word! Born of the struggle, just like birth itself is a struggle."

"And sometimes we don't win…" it wasn't a question.

"If we always won, there could be no winning." He sat back, drinking his coffee, looking thoughtfully upwards, shaping what he wanted to say. "But winning is as illusional as losing, since our birthright – our true birthright – is to be the agents of the right change..."

"The right change..." I said, musing. "Like the Buddha's Right Action?"

"Exactly so," he said. "Which has nothing to do with winning or losing, and may involve the invocation of the simplest action, or even one of deliberate sacrifice... as you so bravely chose to do with our little piece of theatre last week."

He watched while I cringed at the memory... "Two worlds?" he said.

"What?"

"Are you, perhaps, thinking about the choice of ongoing worlds that depended on your decision at that point?"

I thought back to the woman sitting at the table, forced–no, resolved–to carry on holding the world because there had been no other 'right thing' to do...

"You didn't give me much choice," I said, looking into his eyes for something. "Would you have wanted me to–" there it was... the truth. "Didn't it change you, in a small but significant way?"

My voice was a whisper, "Yes."

"Success feeds the ego, unless we watch its effects very carefully," he smiled. "And we spent many coffees talking about the outer rim of the enneagram, which is the world of the ego – to which we shall return, once our quest around this zodiac of labours is done." He drank the last of his coffee. "Did you feel that your heroic gesture of last week fed your ego?"

"No." I answered, truthfully. "It felt like it fed a different part of my 'interior'."

"And you didn't feel you had failed in any way?"

Suddenly, it was there–the picture he was carefully painting, I grasped at it. "No–neither success nor failure... just a sense of rightness, whatever the world might have thought!"

"The world apart from Rose?"

I laughed then, remembering the unlikely partnership that occasionally manifested on the strange stage of our Monday coffee-shop meetings. "Yes... darling Rose." I looked behind me to flash a look of gratitude at the cafe's elderly owner; but she was nowhere to be seen.

"But last week she was there when you needed her?"

"Oh yes…"

And she was completely present to your 'suffering', and came, from nowhere, to stand beside you, offering the most unlikely and exact help…"

I nodded, lost in the bliss of the memory of that help.

"Heracles had a 'Rose', too" John said. "but despite the skill of Nereus the shapeshifter, Heracles never saw the help being offered… Often, it's right in front of us, but we are looking for something else, something the rational mind decides we need for the problem it cannot solve…" He allowed himself a grin. "So, he had to find it through his wanderings around the four directions of his world, eventually discovering the key by not looking for it, but helping someone else…"

I'll swear there was a tear in his eye as he got to his feet, grabbing his raincoat, then kissing the top of my head before striding out into the deluge of a mid-November morning. That and a smile…

Thirty Eight

       I wasn't late, but the object placed ominously in the middle of our table suggested I might be...

"Morning John," I said, warily. "Is this supposed to tell me that time is running out – that I'd better get enlightened quick or you'll pass the time with another acolyte?"

He stared at me, saying nothing, as I digested what I had just uttered... Then, he turned the old-fashioned egg-timer flat on its side, so that none of the sand inside was moving. "Better?" he asked, pleasantly.

"I...I didn't mean..." I muttered, realising how presumptuous I had been. His eyes were dancing with humour, and there was no anger there at all.

"We do things..." he said. "We do things, usually out of some kind of fear, that are knee-jerk reactions, of which we are then ashamed."

He looked at me. I nodded, composing myself and letting the tension go. "It was just that I saw the 'clock ticking' and felt... well, you know–got at!"

He was laughing now, and pointed at the levelled timer. "You'd rather nothing happened at all?"

It was pure mischief but I realised that I had created the whole thing. I reached across and restored the ticking sand. "You were saying," I said, softly. "or, rather, you weren't saying."

"One last look at the third labour," he said, smiling. I realised that the tiny episode was completely gone, that he had moved on – almost as though he spent most of his life observing the strangeness of ego-based reactions in others... and no doubt in himself, as he never professed to be a saint.

I fought to reclaim some high ground. "Gemini, you said? "The twins?"

He nodded, pleased I had remembered the earlier reference which we had not yet discussed.

"What do twins have to do with the trials of Heracles, do you think?"

I thought long and hard. I was beginning to get the 'key' to this way of thinking. Twins could refer to siblings, of course, but they could also refer to things linked at different levels, like a matching or contrasting set of rooms on different floors of a good hotel.

"We are twinned within ourselves," I said, feeling the certainty flow through me in a way that ordinary knowledge did not. "We are twin beings..."

"And the other bit is referred to as the–"

"Soul," I said, ready with the answer, in a way that did not upset the flow of the moment, which I was beginning to see was its perfection. I followed through on the idea that had just come to me. "And we can choose which room we live in, as long as we have enough intent – we can view the world through the eyes of the ego or the eyes of the soul... with a bit of help!"

John laughed, gently, at my finale. "Yes," he said, his eyes filled with kindness. "We all need a bit of help from time to time – but the soul itself will help, we just have to ask it!"

"Knock and it shall be opened unto you..." I said, half dreaming the words from my childhood.

"Exactly so," he said. "This is not a new art..."

I looked down at our table. The sands had all run into the bottom part of the glass figure, which I now realised resembled a lemniscate: the figure of eight symbol of infinity... and probably a host of other things. "Time's up?" I ventured.

"Depends where you want to live; like Heracles, once he had it figured out, you have a choice...and it's really very simple.

I watched his eyes lead mine down to the egg timer. Feeling elated, I pulled it into the air and turned it around.

"And so, like Heracles," he said. "With one action, you have defeated the serpent, by pulling it from its native earth, and established where you want your new home to be."

I looked at the tiny grains of tumbling sand. Whatever I did–unless I laid the object down, sideways again–they would flow. And the flow would always be into the world, like a multi-dimensional field of spiritual gravity – that was, presumably, why we were here. But I could, at any time, raise it up, by inverting the object... just as I could choose to see things from the perspective of the soul – by asking it to fill my life, as the sand grains filled the glass chambers.

For the first time that morning, John picked up his coffee and drank some, smiling at me over the rim of the cup.

I did the same; and we grinned at each other like children.

Thirty Nine

Little furry model animals don't normally do much for me, but this one, placed in the middle of our usual table in the cafe, made me giggle. It had big doe-eyes, the sort you'd see in Japanese comic books. With somewhat smaller eyes, at least proportionately, John was smiling at me from across the table. I took a breath, but Rose arrived with our two lattés before I could speak.

"One of my favourites, this," he said, still grinning like the proverbial Cheshire Cat and stealing the silent pause.

"Because it's my birthday this mythical month?" I asked, somewhat cheekily. He laughed. "The sign of Cancer, the crab; Glorious June…rather far in the future… won't buy you a pressie just yet!" he said, doing his best to copy the deer's eyes and using them to peer, pathetically, out at the dark and wet November morning. Then he added, in response to my mock frown, "Go on then, tell me the story."

"Okay," I said, ready. "Heracles is tasked with capturing a wild fawn, and taking in to the Temple of Apollo, the Sun-god. He finds himself looking at a beautiful landscape. On one far hill, near Apollo's temple, he spies the female deer, but, as he looks at it, the voice of Artemis, the huntress, comes from the disc of the moon, and warns him that the animal is under her protection and that she has nurtured it from its infancy."

"Very good," said John. "Was it Artemis alone who warned him off?"

"No," I answered, "The mighty Diana, the sky huntress dear to the Gods, claimed ownership of the fawn, too. Both said they had guarded it to maturity." As I spoke, John leaned forward, as though listening intently, though there was nothing wrong with his hearing. In so doing, he inadvertently pushed his hot coffee mug towards my left hand, lying flat on the table top. I could feel the heat and my hand moved, automatically, away from the scalding pot.

He seemed not to notice my discomfort. "So Heracles had an easy time of this one?" he said. "He just used his powers to capture the fawn, knowing that the temple to which he was to return the creature was that of Apollo, the greatest of the Gods?"

"No–" I said, conscious that my left hand had again flinched away from something hot. I looked down and saw that his cup was, again, very close to my skin. His eyes were on me, as though boring into my soul. It could only have been a repeated accident, so I continued. "–far from it! The two goddesses spent a year helping the golden-antlered fawn to evade Heracles, despite his great skills."

"But he caught it, eventually?" said John.

"Yes…" I replied. "After a year of trying – it was rather sad. In his exasperation, I presume, he shot at the fawn and wounded its foot, Unable to flee, it was captured and carried by Heracles into the temple of Apollo, and remained there, claimed and healed by Apollo himself, despite the protestations of Artemis and Diana." Suddenly, I became conscious of the burning, again. "Bloody hell!" I exclaimed, "You've got to be doing that deliberately!"

With eyes like a cobra his gaze never left mine, not even looking down as I moved my hand far away from the hot mug to show him what he had been doing. "And what did the fawn symbolise?" he asked, apparently unbothered by my outburst.

There was that funny ringing in my head when he said this. He had set up one of his situations while we were speaking. What was the link between my singed skin and the fawn?

"Did you need to use reason to decide to pull away your hand?" he asked, continuing to look at me intensely.

I was calming down – knowing that there would be a noble motive behind the idiot's actions. "Reason?" I muttered, still hurt with the idea of being burned like this, even though the pain had been slight. "No, of course not – my body knew exactly what to do in reaction!"

"So it did," he said. The intense and unsettling gaze was subsiding. "And the fawn represents that instinctive nature… but this fawn was taken from its natural state, hunted for a year by a hero, shot at the point on its body where it made contact with the earth, and then carried, lovingly, on the breast of

Heracles, into the highest of temples..."

There was a noise in my head that was not a noise but something more profound–more like a beating of wings...Something was opening up. I grasped at what he had said, the slight pain in my little finger forgotten. "So, an instinctive ability, not requiring reason, is hunted, despite the grasp of two goddesses, and, though wounded, successfully delivered to the Sun-god in his temple?"

"Where it heals and is returned to the same hillside on which Heracles first saw it." His eyes had resumed their normal kindly state. The cobra stare had gone. He was now sitting back in his chair, the offending mug transferred to its normal duties.

"So, what was transformed, or rather, re-homed?"

I didn't want him to tell me. I knew this was important. "Can I have a week to think about that?" I asked, watching him smile and nod into the latté.

Forty

It had been quite a week. I had wrested with the challenge that John had thrown down: the nature of the golden-antlered doe in the Heracles story. He had hinted that it was symbolic of something that underwent a transformation in the human being; something that was a key attribute, an ability that developed as an extraordinary kind of skill at a certain point of the spiritual path.

I entered the cafe. Once more he was there before me, folding a large sheet of paper into a complex pattern of triangles. Beside him on the table was one he had finished earlier, which appeared to have six pointy legs holding it upright, in a stance that looked quite formidable, as two of the six were pointed up at me.

"Morning, Alexandra," he said, without taking his concentration from the intense act of paper folding. "Meet Canopus who is a kind of Argonaut," he added, nodding to the six-legged creature which seemed to be staring up at me.

"Isn't that mixing up a whole set of principles?" I asked.

"Sufficient to get us thrown out of most schools of antiquity," he nodded, folding furiously, but flicking his gaze up over my shoulders towards the counter. "But I'm desperate–probable cause: lack of coffee!"

"Here you go, love," said Rose, putting my coffee down next to me with a supportive pat on the shoulder. Then she turned to John, with, "You don't take sugar," as she thumped down his drink, ensuring some of it spilled onto his careful folding. The two sugar sachets were similarly dumped onto his masterpiece.

"Thank you, old friend," replied John, wounded in the manner of the perpetually misunderstood. It was obvious he had crossed some sort of line in his preparation of the 'scene' this day.

"Hope you choke on it!" said Rose, scuttling backwards, but not before she patted me on the other shoulder. Then the room began to shift again, as though her simple gesture in the face of our collective antagonist had opened something up for me to see.

"Strong shoulders, then?" asked John, all innocence, and still intensely busy with his, now, coffee-stained origami. "Strong woman, that Rose," he said, sucking air through his teeth. "Shouldn't want to mess with her..." There was the faintest edge of a smile at the extremities of his tight lips.

Other than 'good morning' I had said nothing since my entry into the cafe. I looked down at the now near-finished pair of objects as John sliced open one of the sugar packets with a finger nail and triumphantly wrapped it around what miraculously became the worst rendering of a crab I had ever seen... but it was, unmistakably, a crab...

Still mute, I sipped the hot coffee, holding it with two hands that seemed to resonate with their supportive 'strong shoulders', and the figure of the crab before me, with its impromptu and highly coloured paper carapace.

"And now it's time for the journey of the crab – or, should we say the journey begun in the time of the crab." With that, he marched the dreadful beast, for which I had developed an unlikely fondness, into the open hull of the coffee-flavoured boat that took up the entire middle of our table.

"Are we missing a Noah?" I asked.

"It's a very good question, but not necessarily helpful," he said.

"Then this is a much more generic crab boat?"

"Yes, he said. "This is a boat that sets sail, like a shepherd begins a long summer journey to move his flock of sheep."

"So the crab is a generic state of mankind?"

"Excellent!" he enthused. "And where do crabs live?"

I was beginning to get it. "They live in two worlds; so, symbolically, they can climb out of a lower one and into a higher." Something chipped away at another part of my shell and more light came in. "From water – instinct and emotion – to the air of the intellect..." my voice had faded to a whisper.

"Great," he said, then added, "Not all philosophers have loved them, mind," He was shaking his head in the general direction of Rose who, presumably, was scowling at his antics from behind the counter. "The Hebrews disliked them so much, they didn't even give them a name… apart from 'unclean'!" He rubbed his fingers into the dirty pile of sugar and twinkled them up over my head.

"Key piece missing, though," he chuckled. "Damned if I can make that from sugar bags and folded newspaper…

I looked up from my intense study of the crab boat to stare at the madman's flicking fingers, with their twinkling coating of sugar.

"You're doing the stars, aren't you–unlikely though it is–you are making a very passible, if lunatic, impression of a night sky arching over a boat with a crab in it?"

I'll swear there was a tear in his eye, as, he lowered his arms and took hold of his well-earned, if slightly spilled, coffee, which, by then, was probably half cold.

"So, put me out of my misery, dear niece," he appealed, beaming a genuinely tender look my way. "and tell me what this is all about?"

I took a deep breath, seeing more and more of the pattern, and composed my thoughts… I owed him a very good answer to that question.

Curiously enough, Rose chose that very moment to arrive with two fresh coffees – and a wet cloth which she used to clean up our table, using surprisingly gentle fingers to raise John's creations out of the way of the all-conquering rag. When she had finished that, she used the cloth to wipe his sugared finger tips, as though he were a naughty child.

It took me a while to realise that she was laughing between the tutting. But, it was a tonic to see him sitting there, helpless, before the force of nature that was Rose, cleaning.

Forty One

"Animals..." I said, just letting it hang in the air.

"Animals?" John replied, playing his favourite 'dead bat'.

Just at that moment, Rose brought my coffee. Getting to our coffee shop after him was becoming annoying–particularly as I made every effort not to. Wherever this myth led, it was clearly important to him that I 'got it'. He had arranged everything to control the quest; and something inside me was rebelling...

"Whatever it is, it's all about animals..." I said, sure that the word 'animals' was the key to unravelling my tangled, but not muddled, thoughts.

I had wrestled and wrestled with this one–the inner meaning of the doe in the sign of Cancer; the doe that three people claimed but... suddenly the review of my own hunt triggered a further thought...

"Hunting... the doe... there was only one hunter!" I blurted out.

"Heracles.." John sipped his coffee, smiling and nodding, "You!" Then he held up his cup so that it obscured part of the one eye he kept open, looking at me with half an eyeball.

"Half an eyeball..." I muttered, disgusted, and becoming sarcastic in my frustration. "Shouldn't take it out on you, but it's still half a sodding eyeball..."

John chuckled. "Took Heracles a while," he said, calmly, "In fact, it took him a whole cycle of the zodiac..."

"And all the time Diana and Artemis tried to frustrate him, hiding the Doe in the eternal forests," I added, remembering the details of the myth, again.

"And did the Sun god, Apollo, intervene?" he asked. It was a carefully phrased question. I wanted to say 'yes' but then thought better of it, because Apollo hadn't really – not till the end.

"Not really..." I sipped my own coffee, watching the hunter that was John gaze at me over the top of his own cup. "It was only when he took the Doe, injured, into the Sun temple, that Apollo intervened, as though…" I had slipped into that state of revelation, again.

"As though…?" asked John, very quietly.

"As though… the Doe were a child of the temple that had to be brought back to where it began," And then I added, "And Apollo healed it so that it was, apart from being captured, unchanged from how it had started – whole, again!"

"And the purpose of all that would be?"

I could feel the 'flow' of the moment–that surge of energy as something new broke into my consciousness.

"To free it from the forces of the Moon–symbolically, the organic forces of evolution, which had done their work." I felt the surge continue, even as he asked me the next question, which I knew would follow.

"And what of Diana, the huntress of the Sun? Why would a daughter of Apollo have to be denied in her claim to the Doe?"

I was ready. "Because Apollo, being the male and Kingly figure, would be the originator, in a spiritual sense the Father, who generated the Doe to be the carrier of something vital for those…" I searched for the word. The male and female aspects of gender did not fit, easily, into modern thinking; but I could see their original intent. "…below."

That was it… something had been 'given' to those below, those evolving from a divine birth–Apollo's offspring, and Heracles had been the only one, apart from Diana's permitted and brief glimpse, to be allowed into the temple of the Sun. But Diana was a principle and not a human. The folded paper creature and the boat from our last Monday's coffee meeting had represented that climb of evolution… So, the divine gift had to be at the heart of what it was to be human; and yet this single thing, this Doe, existed at different levels in all of us, male and female, equally.

"The Doe is our aliveness, then?" I asked it, knowing that I was close, but not sure that it was exactly right.

"And what's the real test of something alive?" John asked, embracing me with his eyes.

"We feel, we think, we react to the world, we create, we suffer, we have joy…"
I was streaming out all that I could think of about what it was to be human.

"All of those, yes," he said. "And so you have to find a single attribute that covers the lowest forms of life right up the highest; something possessed by the simplest single-celled life-form, but which evolves with it, expands with it, to become human and then, as though reaching its maturity in the first two phases of its existence, as the Doe did, teases with its new beauty and dances away, to create a chase, a quest..." My skin crazed with goose bumps as he said the closing word very softly, "Creating a hunt that takes us all beyond being human."

Finishing his coffee, he reached into his black bag and took out three small envelopes. Then he left, kissing me briefly on the top of the head, as he departed.

For a while, I stared at the white rectangles on the table. I would open them on the train... I would descend into my mundane but essential world of London to fight for my living, as animals must do; but, I thought, holding up the three envelopes, I would make sure I looked up at the stars a lot this week...

But, then, I didn't do that... In my impatience, I ripped open the envelopes and shook out three pieces of paper. They were blank on the sides that emerged. With that sinking feeling I turned them all over... blank on the other sides, too.

Cursing him, I left the cafe, but, as I walked, I began to smile. The part-rage had marked a transition from passive to active. He was no longer going to spoon-feed me the answers. I knew I would have to work for it from now on.

The huntress stretched her claws and looked up at the pale winter sun. She was hungry...

Forty Two

I had seldom seen him laugh so much, nor so good-naturedly.

The journey to 'here' had taken several weeks of thought, and I could – finally – see the care with which he had constructed it. On one level it was infuriating; on another–a much deeper one–I was tempted to say it was infinitely beautiful…

In response and some deference to this, I had spent ages with the makeup. A thin layer of jet-black, supplemented by a slightly opaque lacquer, topped off with a tiny starburst picked out in white pencil. Easy enough, you might think, but it took me four attempts and forty-five minutes to get it right.

It would have looked sensational, on, say… a balloon. On a barrister in a pin-stripe suit, walking hurriedly through the unusually busy streets of Morecambe on a wet Monday morning of the last working week before Christmas, it clearly didn't. The five-minute journey from the car park was a lesson in itself… As humans, we're not very good with the unusual. We mistrust it… I don't know whether it's genetic or societal; but something in us is deeply afraid of that which is different… The end of my nose, for example, on that December day. When I entered the cafe, he looked up. I think he had detected my change of mood at the end of last week's meeting. His anxious glance to the door, as I entered, confirmed it. But his face lit up when he took in the visage of the madwoman before him.

"In honour of Rudolf for the colour-blind?" he asked, rocking with mirth in his old wooden chair, which was making ominous creaking noises – Rose was not known for the extravagance of her furniture budget.

"Whatever do you mean?" I asked, mustering innocence and pretending to ignore the curious faces of those around us. Several, for some reason, were regulars at this odd time of seaside day; and for a second which set me blushing, I could have sworn that everyone in the cafe was looking at me…

"Bit of a rush this morning, dearie?" asked Rose, as she brought my coffee. "Lend you a mirror if you like?"

I just smiled at her kindly, understanding her taunt and letting the moment unfold and unveil its potential. I suspected that they both knew that – and that Rose had moved from her customary protective stance to one that said, 'okay then, darling… but, after this, you're on your own…'

Aware that the 'flow' had unspoken power in it, John sipped his coffee and stared at me before speaking.

"So," he said, softly. "As obvious as the black starburst on the end of your nose?" His composure weakened and he nearly spilt Rose's carefully prepared latté. "I assume that this magnificent gesture, in the interests of mutual lunacy, is related to a certain Greek Doe?"

"What little gesture?" I retorted. I hadn't finished with the opening, yet.

He nodded, saying nothing and feeling for the right entry into my mind. The Huntress called Alexandra was still hungry – very hungry.

"Are you saying that there's something wrong with my appearance?" I asked.

"Not 'wrong' with your appearance…" he said. "…simply unusual – though very stylish…" he paused, looking for the right words. "…in its own way." He was still rocking, though playing by my rules – which had become very important in my quest.

It was time to unveil the script. "I can't see anything wrong with my nose, anyway?" I queried, looking him straight in the eye. That's what had taken forty-five bloody minutes to get exactly right – I literally couldn't…

He leaned forward, suddenly conscious that there was a lot more to this than simply Christmas.

"No…" he said. "Of course – how clever!" he sat back and, in the face of my continued silence, I could tell he was thinking on another level about what I had done. "And there is, from your viewpoint, nothing at all unusual about what's on the end of your nose – you literally can't see it!"

And there was the heart of it, I thought… I wondered where he would chase the trail next – as Heracles had to, for a full year, while he pursued the elusive Doe…

He spoke in measured tones, "But I… being well intentioned towards you – as you know," he raised his eyebrows for my confirmation. I gave him nothing.

"might point out that I can see something very unusual at the end of your nose!"

"You mean you are aware of it?"

At that, he leaned back and signalled to Rose that we might need more coffee. She had been standing right behind me, and I would like to say that I could feel her grinning at the power-exchange in the dialogue; but that might be fanciful.

"That's so very good…" he said. "Who knows?"

He had caught it… "Well, I know, that I have an end of nose…" The fresh coffee came, silently. My half drunk one was whisked away, with an intensity that was not hostile. "But, you are telling me that I don't know all there is to know about it?"

"In the sense that a friendly fellow like me… or Rose might?" he nodded to his compatriot in the land of the idiots, before continuing. Rose had re-taken her position behind me, it seemed, though I could see her less than I could see the black and white starburst on the end of my nose.

"Babies don't know they have ends of noses," I said. "They think the pinkness, glimpsed occasionally, belongs to the world. They don't realise that it moves with them and not with that world…"

This was gathering pace, nicely, I thought. I continued, "So they have to become aware of their world first, and then they find, much later on, that the end of their nose projects into it but really belongs to them!"

He sat back, beaming at me. "So, we move from awareness, to knowing… to?"

The claws flexed quickly, out and poised. "Why…" I said, finishing my coffee and making him wait. I stood up to go and planted the customary kiss on his head. "… the end of 'noing', of course!"

When I had parked the car at Lancaster and taken my reserved seat on the train, I thought of them both – and their astonished faces as I left. I was still chuckling as the train left the urban landscape and emerged into the pale green of a Winter's morning; but the claws had long retracted.

"Happy Christmas, uncle John," I whispered; and then silently hugged Rose, too.

Forty Three

I had found the Lion in the window of a charity shop. It was a combination scarf, handbag and, now, hat...

"I'm assuming that's a lion you're wearing?" asked John, when I sat down with my coffee and two butter knives.

"Sorry about that," I replied. "Best I could do – found it in a charity shop and it needed a bit of TLC and a good wash!"

"Washed the stuffing out of it?"

"More or less. I fear its debut will be its swan song, but, heh, it was worth the pound it cost me, just for the look on your face..."

We both sipped our coffees, each looking at the other warily. I liked that–liked that he could no longer predict all my moves. Just to keep him on his toes, I took the knives and crossed them over each other in the middle of the table, so they were shaped like a St Andrew's cross.

"We're having hot cross buns?" he asked, knowing we weren't, but little else.

"Do we usually have hot cross buns?" I asked, unreasonably.

"A very confined fencing match, then?"

I chuckled. "To the death then..." It was the only sense I could make of the myth – that it was a fight to the death, only one of them could win... Heracles or the lion.

He looked exasperated. Oh good, I thought.

Not wanting to give more away without him having to work for it, I kicked him a snippet. "A fight to the death, then..."

John looked up from reading the back of his coffee cup. "Ah, a fight... so we are doing the Nemean Lion?"

I didn't mean to gush at that point but the sheer frustration of trying to fathom the myth had got to me. "Yes, we are... and it's a sod!"

"I'll grant you it's not obvious..." he said, looking like he really did want to help.

I'll give him that – his youthful propensity to sulk, remembered from my teens, had diminished with age.

"It's less than obvious–its despicable," I said. "A fearsome lion terrorises a region of the county, Heracles is told he must kill it. He discards all the weapons he's been given, except the club he made himself. Finally, he corners it in a cave – but the cave has two entrances so the lion keeps escaping. To reduce his chances to zero he lays down even his club and enters the cave with no weapons, strangling it with his bare hands... job done."

"Are we getting a little frustrated with Heracles on this one?"

I was tense, he was right. I could find no meaningful start point for decoding this myth.

"Want a clue?" he persisted.

I nodded, then breathed out, noisily, and sipped my coffee. Rose appeared and John signalled we might need two more.

"Saviours were often described as being born in caves..." John said.

"Saviours..." I mused. "But isn't Heracles the Saviour?"

"Well, yes, of course," he said. "But is Heracles singular."

"Of course," I said, engaging mouth before brain. "There's just one of..." and then I saw it – saw that Heracles was, of course all such figures; all aspirants on this path. I looked up to see John smiling, warmly, at me. "Born in a cave..." I whispered. "Like you know who.."

"Like many such you know whos." he said.

"But he wasn't born in that cave, he just went in after the Lion – after lighting a fire at the other end to block it!"

It was obvious I had lost my 'edge' with this one. Nothing was connecting as it had before the previous visit.

"And in how many ways are people said to be 'born'?" He smiled and took the new coffees from Rose.

I sat up, catching the edge of the meaning he was trying to convey. "So, something happened in the cave; something that Heracles had to do in the 'darkness of an interior?"

John winced at hot coffee taken too soon. "Now you're getting somewhere!"

"But why fight a lion – apart from the obvious?"

"I think you need to go and look up lions," he said. "Or I'll end up telling you the whole thing and spoiling it…"

I nodded at this wisdom. For once, we drank and laughed and exchanged small talk.

"Bring Leo back with you next week," he said as he kissed me on the paw…

Forty Four

I brought the lion scarf-gloves-hat back with me on the next Monday, but tied it up, neatly, in a wide, red, ribbon. I placed it on the table before John arrived. It and his coffee were waiting for him on arrival.

He smiled as he sat down and took in the tabletop. "Tied it yourself?" he asked with a twinkle in his eye.

"All my own work…"

"Bet you could do it blindfold?"

"Well, in dim light, at least," I replied, sure that I had, finally, fathomed the inner meaning of the myth of the Nemean Lion.

"Did it struggle?"

"Put up one hell of fight… nearly cost me my life!"

"Lions are like that – all or nothing, really!"

"But strangely linked with our destiny… and our past, too."

"Symbol of courage in much of mythology," he said, widening his smile. I could sense the trap.

"But not here…" I just let the words fall onto the table top.

"Wasn't Heracles courageous?" he asked.

"Very much so, but he wasn't fighting a lion…"

"He wasn't?" John sipped his coffee and feigned surprise.

I drank my own and chose my words carefully. "Leo, here–" I smiled. "–very clever that little throw-away as we were leaving, last time…" I sipped some more coffee, making him wait. "Leo here isn't a Lion… he's a self…"

"Which self?" His eyes had become as hard as diamonds, sensing the end of the chase.

"The Leonine self – the one that wants to be centre stage, like the star sign… the ego."

"Oh…" he said, twinkling again and grinning behind the raised coffee cup.

"Ohhh, that one."

"But you didn't kill it?" he said, nodding to the pile of wool trussed up in bright red.

"There are days when I might fancy eating a villager!" I said, reasonably.

He nodded. "So, you don't need to kill it, but as far as the world is concerned it's dead?"

"Exactly. As long as I can look at it, tied up in red, and remember its nature, then I know I have it tamed..."

And then something else came to me, something that completed the sequence of meaning and wrapped it up, neatly, with my captive combo before us. "... and I could just carry on wearing it, of course, but in a way that showed I was only wearing a lion's skin, not being one..."

"Clever that..." he said, looking at the captive Leo and nodding to Rose as she approached, smiling, with our next round of coffees.

Forty Five

I was trying hard to hide my annoyance but I could tell he knew.
"Difficult one?" he asked me, but smiling at Rose as she deposited our coffees, none too gently, on one of the side tables – our usual had been taken by some non-regulars… the nerve!

"More like all the discarded out-takes from the other myths" I muttered.

"You can learn a lot from out-takes," he offered, looking reasonable and calm and generally hateful.

"Not from this lot!" I moaned, then was immediately ashamed of myself.

"Why don't we just play with the out-takes, then?" he asked, watching me sigh and let out the tension whose source was less than obvious. I had come far in the past few weeks; I didn't want to blow it, now.

I sat back; drank a minute's worth of coffee and composed myself. "Okay," I began. "Heracles has to retrieve something called the Girdle of Hippolyte." More coffee, then, "Hippolyte is an important Queen who rules a land by a great sea, the home of all the women in the known world – no men to be seen, at all!"

"Kind of Amazons, then?" John asked.

I held my hands up and rolled my eyes in gesture of unknowing, then took a breath before continuing, "The women worship around their beloved Queen in a temple of the moon, but, once a year, they go off to have a party with some unnamed men…" It was sounding preposterous, but, as far as I knew, that had been a true account so far…

I gathered together what I had studied about the rest of the myth and finished my coffee.

"The Queen is forewarned of his approach at the same time that Heracles is given his mission–to take the Queen's Girdle, whatever that was in ancient times…"

"A magical girdle, I should think," said John. "Probably had special properties..." He looked at me for a reaction, then let it go, continuing, "Parents are usually important, whose daughter was Hippolyte?"

"Well, there's another strange thing!" I said, a certain and mysterious enthusiasm for my task germinating. "Despite all the womanly focus, Hippolyte was a daughter of Mars–Ares, I should say..."

John leaned forward to speak, "The most physical of the Gods of War!" he said. "A very strange combination, especially when you think that the other God, or should I say Goddess, of war was Athena – she of the wise owl..."

I looked at John, fixing his eyes. "As though anyone could choose their parents?"

John held my stare. "Oh, but the creators of myth certainly did choose the parents..."

My mind changed gear, seeing the chasm of what I had missed. "Of course... they are not people at all, they're parts of us, principles..." I sighed.

"And did the Queen of all these men-less women give the magical girdle to Hercules?"

"No!" I blurted. "Well, yes and no... She was ready to give it to him, but, ignorantly, he fought to take it off her and killed her in the process, thereby killing the mother of the sacred child..."

John finished his coffee. "Sounds serious to me, killing the Queen, who is the mother of the sacred child?"

My mood had become sombre. "Does, doesn't it?" And then I remembered that this story of Heracles had a further ending. But I knew it was getting late. I looked at my watch and stood up to go, giving my closing speech.

"But Heracles was seen to redeem himself, later, by fighting his way into the innards of a sea monster that had eaten the sacrificed Hesione, wife of the Trojan, Priam, rescuing her in her hour of greatest need and balancing the scales of his life."

John nodded as we both headed for the door. It had been a complex and unsatisfactory half hour. "Yes," he said. "he was seen to redeem himself, though the mother, the Queen of the sacred child, was dead... and the women of the land by the sea were leaderless."

He opened the door for me. "And you got the introduction slightly wrong," He

142

said.

"I did?"

"Yes. Hercules didn't get his instructions about the girdle from his teachers, those instructions – the surrender of the magical girdle – were sent directly to Hippolyte. All Heracles did was to arrive at the edge of the watery kingdom, where the moon was worshipped, by women, alone; and where the god of war was sacrificed to, by a Queen who wore the girdle of love and was the key to the generation of the sacred child." he paused for breath, smiling at how much he was trying to put into his closing words. "Was Hercules really active, apart from killing someone who was likely to meet his greatest need?" I was stunned by this summing up. Just before he crossed the busy road, he laughed and shouted back over his shoulder.

"Oh and don't forget that all this takes place in the month of Virgo!"

And then he was gone... and I was left with an old file full of very confusing out-takes...and only a week to make sense of them...

Forty Six

"I'm not sure, but I think it centres around the child," I said, as Rose brought our coffees.

John looked thoughtful–so thoughtful he sipped his coffee prematurely and burned his top lip.

"Ouch!" he grumbled, obviously hurt. "Sod it..." He bent to put the overly-full coffee cup down, but it slipped in his fingers at the last minute and some spilled onto the table. He looked, speechless, at the result. "Made a hash of that, then," he muttered, mopping up the spillage with his napkin.

I stared at him and laughed. He was normally so controlled. "Unlike you, that!" I said.

"Go on," he said, ignoring me, He licked his burnt lip and frowned. "I agree; the child is very significant... and Heracles, is he significant?"

I considered the question; how could the central character not be significant? "Well, he just makes a mess of the whole encounter with Hippolyta, doesn't he?"

"Yes he does," said John. "But, technically, he achieves his goal?"

"He does, but..." I responded, leaning forwards. "...and this seems to be at the heart of it–he treats it like a military mission and completely misses the most subtle parts of it, even though the Queen of the Amazons had already decided to help him, and all he had to do was accept the gift that was waiting– a gift he really needed!"

John nodded and blew on the top of his diminished coffee, taking no chances this time. "And he realises that he's done it all wrong and that the doing of it was just as important as achieving the goal; he knows that he shut out so many benign possibilities in the way he acted..."

"But he redeems himself by saving Hesione and, eventually passes on to the next labour?" I asked.

"He does," said John. "but with a heavy heart, as he had once before, remember?"

The image of the wild mares came back to me – the sad death of Abderis through Heracles' neglect of his younger friend's plight. "Are they connected?" John looked at me over the surface of his, now shallower, steaming drink. "Very much so, I would say..."

"As though he is beginning a new stage of his spiritual training!" The image had flashed into my mind, un-thought, from somewhere deeper. The feeling startled me... and then I chuckled, with what felt like a tiny stream of joy. I blurted out, "Mission! It's all wrong era-wise, but the word I used is the key– he's completed his basic training as a disciple and now has to move on to something more fundamental, something deeper, something that really changes lives."

"Like a fresh cup of coffee?" said John, his eyes twinkling with delight at my breakthrough and smiling at Rose when she offered. In times gone by I would have found the trivialising gesture irritating, but now I could see that it contained a lot of love, that he was using it to carry me to the next waypoint in my revelations.

"So, where does Heracles 'go' next?" he asked, then added, conspiratorially, "You've already said it..." He rolled his hands, urging me to keep up the momentum.

"The Child..." I whispered it, not sure of its full implications, but knowing it was right.

"The Child, yes," repeated John. "And how do you make a child?"

"Well, apart from the first bit," I smiled at my absurd reduction. "you have to be a woman!" The words were out before I realised their significance. "The Amazons–" I said. "They were all women, of course, specifically emphasised in the story; and their Queen could make the Child because she had the girdle; which bestowed love and triumph through adversity."

John was grinning at me with something like glee in his eyes. Rose had placed the tin tray with our fresh coffees on the small table and was also smiling.

"Weren't they warriors, too?" John asked. "Hence Ares – Mars?"

I was getting excited with the chase. "So, these warrior women are special in that they can undertake, through their Queen with her girdle of Venus, the generation of a special Child?"

"Yes," said John. "But only the Queen comes out to meet him, by the side of that Great Sea. Not understanding, he kills her in the struggle for the magical girdle which was to be bestowed on him, anyway…"

"So what does he do now?" I asked, quietly, breathing over the new, hot coffee.

"Ah," said John, doing the same. "It depends on who's got the girdle doesn't it?"

Forty Seven

"Another confusing one to make sense of – yes, I know!" said John, looking at my slight scowl, as I sat down to the freshly brought coffees. "But, as we've seen, re-telling the story can help to prompt the right questions…"

I had no idea where the sudden angst had come from. He never put me under any pressure; just made suggestions that, usually, opened a door in my own thoughts. Why was this one different? I sipped some of my coffee and traced the feeling of unease… And then it was there, and easy to define…

"Killing people – Heracles is always killing people!" I said, with some vehemence. "I know he's not a real human, but, honestly, if he was he'd be locked up as a psychopath by now!"

"Yes, ancient wisdom tales tend to be violent… but are the victims really people?" John asked, smiling. "And emotion is good, by the way–it releases energy for our use, hopefully not for violent purposes!"

He drank some more coffee, blowing over the surface to cool it, and appearing to smile, ruefully, at the memory of last week's burnt skin. "So who dies?" he asked.

I took a slow breath, letting the unwarranted anger subside; then began, "Heracles' task is to capture the Erymanthian Boar, which has savaged an unnamed part of the country." I thought for a moment, because the re-telling had triggered another link. "In some myths, the boar – one down from the lion in the hierarchy of admired 'beasts', attacks vineyards, a pristine image of cultivation."

John nodded, "And is that it – that's all he has to do?"

"Not quite," I said. "Confusingly, he is also told to ensure he takes the time to 'eat' as well, suggesting that this task is going to be a breeze."

"And is he armed?" asked John.

"That's a good point," I replied." No less a person than Apollo gives him a new bow, but, in some versions, he leaves it behind because he feels it will increase the chances of him killing, again – a mistake he's determined not to repeat..." I snorted "... as though that made a difference once the wine got into his head and he starts swinging that deadly club of his!"

"Another use of a blunt instrument, then?" John said, smiling at me before continuing with, "Wine? Who did he drink wine with?"

"With Pholos, a centaur – half man and half horse," I replied. "But the wine was neither his nor Hercules' to drink."

John widened his eyes, "Whose wine was it, then?"

"It belonged to all the centaurs–a gift of the Gods– and only to be drunk when they were gathered together."

"So why did Pholos allow it to be drunk?"

"Because Hercules was half mad with the smell of it, and Pholos didn't want to be inhospitable with the famous warrior... perhaps?" I replied, trying to think on my feet. "And Chiron, another famous and wise centaur joined them in the party, after pointing out that they were acting against the rules!"

"But, Heracles was there to catch the wild boar, wasn't he?"

"Yes," I answered, "And after the brawl wherein he murdered the two friendly centaurs, who were only drinking with him, he did so, by setting a trap high on the mountain near the snow line – and proceeded to show off by walking the boar down to the town by holding its hind feet and making it descend on its front limbs..."

"Hmm," said John.

"Oh come on, uncle John, do one of your summaries for me... throw me a few clues!"

"Wily niece..." he said, narrowing his eyes and draining his coffee. "Still.... think Libra, the month of this Labour, and also think of the related symbol of the blindfold woman set tall and apart, holding the scales. Why is she blindfold? Is it just that 'justice is blind'? Think of the two centaurs he killed under the influence of the wine, who were they? Did either of them have a prior relationship to Heracles? Think about the way Heracles captured the boar – was it his usual club led style? Also, remember that Libra is the seventh month of the zodiac. What changes in the movement from six to seven?"

He looked at the empty cup of coffee and, clearly considering another, sighed.

"No… got to go," he said, getting up and kissing me on the top of the head as he had since I was a child. "Most of all, remember that I don't have all the answers… there may not be definitive answers to the myths, as their creators are long gone… but their other-worldly skill is written in the tales. Always remember that, – they were meant to do something to the opening mind…"

He was just opening the door when he called back, "And did he eat?" I turned to look at him, then laughed. "No, actually, he didn't. He got drunk, instead…" I mused on that and watched him leave. I knew I'd miss the old curmudgeon during the coming week.

Forty Eight

"I can see you're brimming with ideas," said John, looking at me slyly, over the rim of his coffee cup. "But perhaps you've not connected them all?" He was right. But I sensed an uncertainty in him, too, about the myth of the boar. As though it still held much that he hadn't been able to fathom. This made me feel better, so I launched into the well-filled, but unconnected islands of meaning I had been able to glean.

"Well, firstly, the whole myth is to do with balance."

He nodded. "Safe ground, I think… and Libra is most definitely about balance, justice being a result of seeing things from that state…"

"An inner state – she's blindfold." I breathed out some of the tension. It annoyed me when I got screwed up about something so trivial… but was it? Were these things of myth not the very terrain of our inner lives?

"Heracles loses one kind of balance – he gets drunk in Pholos' cave," I said. "Intoxicated might be a better word, I've no idea why…"

"An abuse… a poisoning of the natural faculties?" John offered. "or a loosing of the ordinary consciousness, and the opening of an inner state? You could justify both but remember that the wine was a gift to the Centaurs from Dionysus…"

I nodded, "And yet certain symbols are repeated in the myths, which suggest a common, inner meaning, possibly depending on the context?"

"Yes, definitely," he said

Growing in momentum, if not confidence, I continued, "And yet wine–and the vineyards that produce it, are revered as spiritual symbols, too?"

"They are, indeed," he smiled. "So much so, that the red wine is directly equated with the very blood of Christ by the church…" He paused, reflecting. "…and the inner meaning of wine is a higher form of understanding–higher than stone or water which came lower in its scale, so to speak…"

"But this wine causes him to kill two of his most loyal companions – the Centaurs!"

"Who are?" asked John, leaning forward as he did when we were narrowing in on something important.

"Who are half men and half horse."

"And we've met horses before, have we not?"

"Oh yes," I said seeing a chink of light in the cave ahead... or was it an oncoming train..."The wild mares, which Heracles had to tame... symbols of uncontrolled thoughts, as I recall?"

"Yes," said John. "So we can assume that Centaurs, who we will meet again, have a significance in their upper and lower arrangements?"

"In many ways the perfect outer form," I whispered. "I often wish I could have the stamina of a horse to carry me around the weary streets of London..."

"And in a sense you do, with your wonderful legal mind – the product of all its training and discipline?"

I thought about that. And the Centaurs were a good force in the land of Heracles, and he had killed them because he had become intoxicated with something he craved – the lower form of wine. I continued to give voice to my thoughts, lost in an internal reverie, "And this wine was meant to be drunk only by the Centaurs, when together, in a form of communion!"

Which, presumably, lifted them, as good communion does, to a higher place within themselves–and collectively."

I felt a rush of love for the Centaurs, and looked forward to a future reunion with them. They seemed to be wise beings, perhaps more limited than Heracles in potential, though not in pub behaviour..."

He smiled. "They've always had a place in my heart, too."

"It's a battle for balance, then," I said, getting enthusiastic. "fought in two arenas – the place where the wrong wine can intoxicate to the point of killing friends who are the epitome of balance; and the high ground where the only way to catch the unregenerate animal is with artifice – the right use of the mind..."

"And Heracles triumphs?" asked John.

"Well, yes..." I responded, sensing that I had the inner grasp of the thing, if not the right words to describe it. "...by humour as much as anything else. He drives the exhausted animal down the mountain and amuses all below with the spectacle." I sipped the last of my coffee, lost in my thoughts. "Perhaps he turns it into a parody by making it human-like, while showing that it can never be so…"

"It could even be a visual apology to the Centaurs," John said, "showing a man atop the wild beast of the boar – a lesson learned?"

He watched me cross the last few feet of my mental process.

"He triumphs by being human, within which, by the grace of something very high, all things are forgiven, once wisdom is grasped…" I fell silent.

"Sometimes, you astonish me…" said John, ordering two celebration coffees from a smiling Rose, who, strangely, was just passing our table.

Forty Nine

"Scary stuff!" said John, smiling at my carefully planned opening. I carried on using my twisting hand and wrist to greet him, as though both were parts of a snake.

"Okay...enough," I said, feeling my wrist muscles start to ache, "And I know I'm eight of them short..."

"Need some hydration?" he asked, with a cheeky grin, passing me my latté.

I broke into a laugh at the play on words. "Funnier that it should have been," I chuckled.

"So..." said John, wringing his hands in mock delight. "Tell me about the Hydra and what part it played in the spiritual education of Heracles."

"Well, then..." I sipped my hot coffee, savouring Rose's skills with the old Italian machine which chuntered in the corner near the entrance to the kitchen. "It's quite a simple one: Heracles has to locate a nine-headed snake monster–the Hydra–and kill it... more killing..."

"Perhaps 'slay' might be better?"

"Slightly different meaning?" I queried. "More righteous, perhaps, less gratuitous?"

John nodded. "I think so. Less like cold-blooded or drunken murder?"

"Yes, that's good..." I drank some more coffee and decided that 'slaying' felt better.

"And there are nine heads to the beast, so you're on home ground?"

It was obvious what he meant–the Greeks' choice of nine 'heads' mapped perfectly onto the enneagrams of personality. But the enneagram hadn't been around back then, though a nine-sided figure called the enneagon was a known form. "Is it that simple?" I asked.

"I think we are entitled to take that short cut." he replied. "As serious students of the nine divisions of the human personality, we get a free ride on this one...

Know any more Greek nines that might help us justify that stance?"

"Just the Nine Muses," I said. "Inspiration for most of the creative activities, from poetry to song to dance to astronomy..."

"One for a different day, then," John said, "But it all adds up to the fact that the Greek philosophers believed that there were nine facets, over many dimensions, to the human soul..." He drank some of his coffee, looking pensive. "So, where did he find the Hydra?"

"In a swamp," I said; then realised my mistake as I noticed his smile. "In the lowest part of the psychic anatomy of himself..."

John inclined his head in agreement, "Much better," he said, "and did he just stumble over the creature?"

I thought about that, seeing through the myth with the help of his prompting. "No, he had to send flaming arrows into the swamp to get the Hydra to reveal itself!" The imagery was suddenly startling, "So he had to shine light-consciousness down into the depths of his being..."

"Very good. And did the Hydra put up a fight?"

I thought about the image of Heracles wrestling a losing battle with the Hydra. "A hell of a fight... Every time Heracles cut off one of the heads, another two grew in its place."

"Like attacking a weed that's ready to drop its seeds!"

"Just like that," I smiled. "And he only won the battle when he remembered some paradoxical advice that he should 'kneel to grow'. "

"He knelt before the Hydra?" said John, looking horrified.

"Only so that he could pull the thing up by its roots, instead of attacking its weedy blossoms," I said, flippantly.

"So he won by taking it from its source of energy?" asked John.

"Yes, by holding it up to the light – or fire in some versions – the heads died and the creature that was the Hydra perished; or rather; became a single immortal head that Heracles buried deep in the mud, in case he ever needed it..."

"And what would he use it for?" asked John, leaning forward.

"To use its vast energy in a 'sober' manner." I said, replaying the dominant image from our last week's conversation. He smiled at me with warmth.

"I'd say we could move on to slay something else now, wouldn't you?"

Fifty

I was ready when he arrived, fifteen minutes early to my twenty. My notebook was out on the small table, already open at the furiously scribbled summary. Two other objects were concealed beneath it. My carefully timed pair of coffees were just being delivered by Rose.

"Gotta hand it to the girl," said Rose, tousling what is left of John's hair as he bent to sit and could, therefore, do nothing about it, "Her timing's getting a lot better…"

John grinned at the twin assault – one on his endangered vanity; the other directed at his habit of keeping me off-guard by being early to these meetings. But he said nothing.

I sipped my hot latté and did my snaky look at him. Still he said nothing.

"I have decided," I began, brimming with plan, "That I need to recover some ground." More coffee, then, "Having valiantly gained the initiative a few weeks ago, I have," I pulled a face, "Lost the plot, somewhat…"

His smile broadened, but he remained, steadfastly, silent.

This was going well. "I had been considering things blow by blow, episode by episode," I said, "whereas I should have been taking Heracles' 'year' as a whole, single process – particularly the astrological significances."

He finally spoke, "There's only so much one can absorb on each visit. More is revealed each time… as it should be!"

He chuckled into his coffee, remembering how hot Rose made it and blowing it first, then sipping it gingerly. "And if you think Heracles is a challenge you should see the frown lines Noah's Ark can induce!"

He sat back again, spreading his arms in a gesture of invitation.

We only had a forty-five-minute window and I had a lot to say. I began, "The astrological progression is really a 'container' for the experiences of the aspirant. He or she begins, as does the astrological year, in March, in the sign of Aries."

John was nodding, waiting.

"He bursts into his quest, ready to head-butt anything, full of the energy of new beginnings. Indomitable Soul that he is, he conquers the wild mares but then leaves his younger and less capable friend, Abderis, alone with the Mares and he is killed. In other words, it needed both Soul and Personality to tame the Wild Mares, and Heracles forgot that…"

I watched his lips break into an approving half smile, but he kept most of it suppressed.

Momentum. I was on a roll. A small sip of coffee and we were off onto the next bit. "In Taurus, he has to deal with the powerful lower nature of his physical self – with instincts, particularly sexual energy, delivering the bull to the care of a benign face of very focussed folk called Cyclopses…" I smiled, "…and points of single focus are very important as we'll see when we get to Sagittarius, our latest foray…"

I was enjoying myself and had no intention of stopping. "He delves into that paradox of soul in body in Gemini, too, but becoming aware that his nature is twin, and that he has to accept that a new world is opening up."

John was passive, smiling and sipping his drink. He made no attempt to speak, enjoying my charge.

"In Cancer," I continued, "he has to come to terms with the fact that he is a member of a family, a tribe, a nation and that these arenas have other souls in them, too; but he doesn't lose sight of his true quest, and achieves the capture of the elusive doe of intuition – proof of the existence of another realm if you ever needed it!"

"He keeps his eyes on the Sun." suggested John, interrupting for the first time. I thought about that and agreed. "Yes, despite the forces of the moon – the personality – being in his way, he achieves his goal."

More coffee, then, "In Leo, there's a fight to the death with the Lion – but only so that something else can be born in the months that follow. In Virgo he makes a complete hash of the gift of new life offered by Hippolyte, the Queen of all the women, who, in a higher sense he should have united with rather than indulging his nasty habit of killing those he loved!"

Note to self, I thought. Stop obsessing about Heracles the butcher… "Comes with being a criminal lawyer," I muttered into my coffee. John pretended not to notice. I continued, "So in Virgo he becomes conscious that the world of form – our physical world, is really nurturing something very special – something belonging to the Sun... or was that Son?" I let the words hang, proud that I had added them off-script, so to speak.

John had finished his coffee. I had barely started mine. He signalled Rose for two more. I smiled at his optimism, my thoughts unspoken, and continued, "In Libra, he has to find the balance of power and the use of the mind to tame the respected but feared Boar, and nearly stalls in his quest, stuck between the forces of the above and the below." I paused. "And then we come to Scorpio – my rising sign..." I sighed.

"Scorpio?" John asked, studying me. "A problem?"

"Sex and death..."

"Beg pardon?"

"My best friend, who is a Scorpio, used to describe her life as a maze of 'sex and death'."

"Nasty sting!" John pulled a face, obviously re-living a distant memory. I didn't ask.

"Where Heracles has to go right down into the muck to pluck out and hold up the Hydra of illusion, thereby separating it from its swampy roots and killing it for good... or did he just show that it was all the same stuff – water?"

"Phew..." said John, pretending to wipe his forehead. "Which brings us to Sagittarius, a noble sign if ever there was one!"

"The archer on a white horse, or another Centaur, if you like, depending on whether you like your twin beings Divine and Human or Human and Animal." I could see that John wanted to add something important. I waved him on.

""Now I saw heaven opened, and behold, a white horse' – Revelation," said my uncle. "The King of Kings comes forward from heaven on a white horse..."

"To bring war and peace, as he does with the deadly Stymphalian birds."

"And how does he defeat them?" Asked John.

"He used a set of cymbals, given to him by Athena, the Goddess of wisdom, to make a vibration–a pure noise so powerful that they were driven away for good."

John leaned forward for his killer question, "So, if the wild mares were really untamed thoughts, what did these dangerous and noisy birds represent?"

I pulled the notebook to one side and looked at the old pocket watch I had left open on the table, sitting on the card. He had not noticed it.

I had timed it to perfection. I left what remained of my coffee and stood, bending to kiss the top of his surprised head in a mirror of our usual goodbye. But he wasn't expecting the finger that sealed his questioning lips.

As I left the cafe, exactly twelve minutes early, I looked back, just once, through the cottage-style windows. He was looking at the watch, and the folded half of the butterfly card I had left beneath it.

As I turned to cross the road, I'm sure I saw a half-smile on his silent face.

Fifty One

When I was younger I did some flying lessons. They began as 'Try Out Day' gift for one of my birthdays, and developed into an expensive hobby which I had to give up when I took out a mortgage on my midweek apartment in London.

As soon as I experienced the sheer joy of the Carnforth Flying School's venerable Cessna taking off from its old grass strip near our home, I was hooked. Climbing, steeply, into the air and seeing the landscape falling away, below, was like entering a new world – one quite different from a trip in a commercial plane: scrubbed nicely clean and sanitised…

Tightly buckled into the small cabin of the Cessna, with my instructor next to me, sharing the intercom link in the headset, was a magical experience.

That was many years ago. There was no coffee in the cabin today, though. And my instructor was no stranger…

"I didn't realise you had become a pilot!" I shouted above the noisy but vibrant engine. "Did you know I had done some flying, too?"

"Yes–you told me, once – many years ago." John took his eyes off the altimeter and smiled across at me. My headset cracked with his voice. "Didn't you stop just before you were due to do your first solo flight?"

I nodded, conserving my throat. There was sadness at the memory; a thing not finished, a road not taken…

"I did some student flying in my thirties," said John, "But it got very expensive; too expensive for our young business to support," he nodded at the memory, his eyes also somewhere far away. "Went back to it when I retired from the IT world. Recently qualified as an instructor!"

"So what's all this got to do with Prometheus and Heracles?" I said.

John looked down through his side window. We were levelling off from our steep climb and turning Westwards.

"Notice how the worlds change; how 'lived in' become a 'map from above'?" he said, ignoring my question.

"You couldn't have a coffee with someone up here in the air!" I laughed, getting his drift. "Unless you were in the same plane..."

John smiled at that. "I've brought a flask, but I'm saving the coffee for something special."

I turned to look at him, but the ironic smile on the lips said that there'd be no more for now... I decided to elaborate on what I knew to be an important connection between the scale of things and their realms, "But down there on the ground, where the view is much more local and small-scale, there are people drinking at Rose's Cafe."

Morecambe was just coming into view on the horizon, the early sun catching the tops of the taller buildings, making golden shards out of the faded glory of the old seaside town. It was beautiful...

"Which way then? Your choice!" asked John, levelling the plane off at our cruising altitude, somewhere over the small town of Kirby Lonsdale. Far below there were a multitude of tearooms, I thought, smiling to myself, but we wouldn't be visiting them, either.

He never wasted an opportunity. I knew the choice of direction was a metaphor. "Pick what to do...a bit like Cerberus, then – the three headed dog? The one that guards the entrance to Hades?"

He laughed at my artifice. "Three heads, three choices?" he said. "And I like 'guards'. Go on then...the enigma of the three headed dog that stops dead people leaving?"

"One of the central issues of our lives – the trap of Desire!" I said over the resonant boom of the engine and its whining thrum-thrum.

He banked us slightly left, taking us onto an easterly course. The line of the distant ocean was a field of gold, lit from the dawn sky behind us. "And the other two heads?"

"The left is sensation, the right, 'good intentions'. They all have snakes wrapped around them...symbols of Illusion, I believe?"

John nodded. "Very good," he said, levelling us off with the shining gold dead ahead. "And does Heracles attack the Sensations or the Good Intentions?"

"Neither!" I laughed, over the whining notes. "He strangles the middle one –

Desire, itself, with his bare hands," I'd had another flash of inspiration and added, "and thereby frees himself…and all the other dead people, if you think about it…"

"Like Buddha, then – he attacks the cause not the symptoms…" John was smiling so much, his teeth were catching the gold of the sun, too. "Wonderful stuff! All yours, then…"

He sat back and let go of the controls. The Cessna's nose began to dip, slightly – he hadn't trimmed for level flight; probably deliberately!

"No!" I screamed into the dawn. But my hands reached out and took the controls as the old memories and skills came back to aid me.

"The Carnforth field is on 120 degrees, over there." He pointed into the golden air. "You can set her down on your own–you can fly us to the underworld…"

My mind was racing, but strangely, there was a sense of calmness; of purpose, there too. "Where's the wind?" I shouted into the mike.

"Coming straight off the sea, I would say, right in line with our approach to the strip… you've been blessed with the perfect approach!" He looked around us then clicked on his radio link. "Charlie-Victor-Delta-Hotel forty-two…final…"

"Roger Charlie-Victor-Delta-Hotel forty-two. Cleared to land." Crackled the almost instant response. Were they all in on it? I wondered.

"Damn you, uncle John," I muttered, loud enough to be heard in his headset. He chuckled. "Very appropriate that… besides, you seemed keen to take the controls."

I was about to object, violently. when I realised he was talking metaphorically. Yes, sod it, I had pushed to take the 'controls'; and had obviously seemed ready to go 'solo' even if he was next to me in the cabin… I wondered… Maybe one was never alone in the cabin of life, just not used to conversing with a loving intelligence that always sat next to us…

The landscape was getting bigger, houses and churches were becoming clearer, below, in all their detail. I recognised the height, the speed the distance… I was doing it right…

About a half mile out from the small grass airstrip, which I could now see, there was a sudden flash of red and gold below us. I looked down and, for a second, I'll swear I could see a tiny shadow of the plane in the gold-licked metal of the Glasgow to London train as it flashed by at a huge speed.

Then there was no more time to think, just to act. "Flaps to twenty," I said pushing the throttle back in, and trimming the plane as we coasted over the edge of the field and seemed to hang in the air, sinking very gently to land with a noisy series of bumps.

The Cessna quickly lost her speed on the grassy runway. With a simple, "I have control." John upped the revs and taxied her off the runway and onto a remote part of the boundary, while I sat, numbed and looking straight ahead, silent and happy in a way I could not find words for.

I came to in the now silent cabin, at the smell of coffee being poured from a flask. The aroma filled the small space, along with another, less expected smell. I turned around to see him holding a steaming plastic mug out to me. In his other hand, he had a miniature bottle of cognac.

"The cognac's for my cup of coffee," he said with a chortle.

"Why?" I whispered, feigning outrage.

"Because I'm preserving your liver," he said, chuckling…

Fifty Two

It was still dark, though the light from the East was streaming into the cold, blue, air. The two take-away cups of coffee looked disappointing. Not because I could already see their contents, but because they weren't from Rose's cafe.

"Last week we were flying over North Lancashire and now the edge of an old market?" I said. My halo was slipping... The previous week's extraordinary events had left me on such a high that I wanted my local magician to conjure up something wonderful and life-changing, again.

"Down to earth with a slump?" He smiled at me, looking very tricky. "Do we only find the life-changing up there?" he waved his coffee cup, perilously, at the sky.

Behind us, Sid, the local fishmonger, was hosing down the outside of his stall. People travelled from miles around to buy his fresh fish, bought off the dock and brought up here before dawn each morning from one of the local fishing ports. In Winter the stall was sold out by the time the sun came up. I looked at the assorted organic debris, being flushed into one of the market's wide grids, and fought hard not to pull a face. I loved fish...but the sight of the dead bits did nothing for me.

"Of course not," I said, chided. "I shouldn't be sulking."

"Quite natural, of course," John replied. "One of the dangers with such a 'high' as last time is that it releases a lot of energy that feels like it belongs in that upper realm and not down here..." he tapped a booted toe near a discarded fish head that had escaped from a one of the stall's plastic bins. "...with all the yucky stuff!"

I watched the water hose cleanse the concrete, directed in well-aimed jets that marked out a single whirling motion. "I can see the connection, though," I responded more positively. "The eleventh Labour of Heracles–the Cleansing of the Augean Stables."

"I don't imagine they smelled very good either…"

"Not after thirty years of accumulated dung…no wonder everyone else had failed and people were dying like flies…"

"Heracles was disappointed, too – with his landing from the heights of Capricorn's mountain, freshly lighted – but he rolled up his club and got on with it!"

"I looked down at my pin-striped legal suit, the expensively heeled shoes, and shuddered. "You want me to clean this fish stall in my business clothes!?"

"Not for now…"

My mind screamed, in your dreams fella! But I kept quiet. Not for now implied a breather before we got there. I flipped the fragile top off the cheap cup, burning my hand with the inevitable spill onto my skin. I suffered in silence, not drinking while I cursed.

Sid had an old assistant who was rather infirm. Long years of working in cold conditions, and collecting fish while the world slept, had taken its toll on them both. But Tony was bent and frail, yet, once again, as every day for the past thirty, he came out from behind the tattered, stripey flap and picked up the second hosepipe, ready and willing to conclude the day's business.

"Never a change to that routine," John said, over the steaming coffee, which he, too, had yet to drink. "They are quietly famous – as is the quality of their produce. Day in, day out: drive for fish, sell fish, clean stall, sleep while the world lives…"

Even John looked sad, his eyes filled with compassion at the plight of the elderly man having to work out his life in this never-ending hard and cold labour.

Sid, much younger and fitter, and still unaware of our study, took his own look at Tony and reached for an old flask. "Here, 'Tony" he said, pouring the older man a plastic cup of hot tea. "Have this, before you freeze in that water!"

"What is it?" asked Tony. "Not bloody tea, again. Don't you ever make coffee?" His voice was rough, like gravel. I supposed it went with the life, but there was something of great hardship and pain in the man's demeanour.

"Lost his whole family in a fire many years ago," whispered John, quietly. "Was unhinged for a while, but Sid brought him back and kept him alive…

They've shared this brutal existence ever since; day in, day out…"

"I'm confused about why we're here? How could spirituality change the life of someone like this?"

"Tony?" asked John. I nodded.

"Very easily…" He waited, looking at me as the growing light of the dawn brought our features into clear relief, there in the shadows. "Be with him," he said. "Feel his pain… Bear witness as you would for a brother or sister. Remember Aquarius is the great leveller…and we can't begin to know the nature of the energies that will be flowing into the conscious life on Earth in the years to come."

He stood back, looking at me, waiting for the moment… "You could change his life right now," he said, softly.

Something hit me then. Wave after wave of compassion poured out of me as I took in the two market workers, rubbing their hands in the cold light. I could feel John nodding as I walked the short distance to where Tony stood, holding out my coffee to him. "It's okay," I said into his startled face. "Just a little something for you… and, may I?" I took the hose from him and began to work the spiral patterns of cleaning, just as he had done. For a while I was somewhere else, just watching the water do the work for me, noticing that only my fine shoes were getting dirty from the splashing. The sense of a new state was overpoweringly wonderful. The simple act of helping had liberated me from the expected and into the real.

When I looked up, John was holding the other hose, which he had just taken from a smiling Sid. The younger man also had a new coffee in his hand. For ten minutes, we cleaned the back of the market stall with our waters. As we were leaving, Sid gave me a peck on the cheek, looking as though this happened every day… But I knew it didn't.

We were about to cross the road and back to the seafront, when a gasping man limped up behind us. I turned to see Tony standing behind me, wordlessly holding out a fish wrapped in a single piece of newspaper. I didn't care how much it would mess up my suit; I took it from him with tears in my eyes and kissed his cheek, running my fingers through his dirty hair.

John said nothing as we collected my luggage from the boot of his car at the station. As I was turning to board my London train, he spoke, "We're nearly there…funny thing about giving to those who have nothing – you always end up getting more back…"

With that, he planted his uncle's kiss in his customary fashion, but the hug spoke more loudly that any words could. "Welcome to the world of the lunatic…"

Nearly there… the words ran around my head most of the to the City. Were we? and where had we been headed all this time?

Fifty Three

There was a coffee, a rucksack and a small, red, paper person waiting for me when I arrived at Rose's Cafe that last Monday morning.
But no uncle John…
The coffee was hot, so I knew he had been there. Besides, I could 'feel' his presence, even though he was nowhere to be seen.
My sense of unease grew when I unzipped the black bag – the one he had often brought with him to our coffee meetings. Inside was an envelope with 'Alexandra' written on the front. I sipped some of the hot coffee before sliding my well-manicured thumbnail under the upper edge and slicing it open.
Inside were a standard-class rail ticket to London, a note and a picture of a place I knew well… Its golden dome a familiar landmark of the area in which our legal chambers were situated.
I picked up the red paper person, which was a crude figure, like a child's cutout. For a second, I thought it had fallen apart in my hands. But the three paper people, linked hand in hand, opened, concertina-style; the lowest touching the table with its bouncing arm.
For the next few minutes, I sipped my coffee, thinking loudly. Was he sending me on a treasure hunt? I was, as usual, bound for London, anyway. Had he gone on ahead? Was our final coffee talk to be carried out in a different landscape to the native north?
An hour later, I was speeding south on the Intercity express. I had used his ticket, even though I already had one for the first-class compartment adjacent. I had only done that because I thought it might be a test and he might have boarded the train, unseen, at the same time. My seat had, at least, been reserved… He had been very thorough in his planning. I noted that, my legal mind working overtime to extract the deepest meaning from this strange experience.

I opened John's black rucksack, again, and examined the note. 'The cattle were red,' It said. 'You can make the connections with ease.' I looked at the three red paper people, spread out before me next to my bacon bun, bought from the trolley as it passed, a poor substitute for the full breakfast being served in First. Beneath the reference to the Labour were the words, 'Like Heracles, seek the blazing Sun.'

In his final Labour, corresponding to the astrological sign of Pisces, Heracles faces a task from which he may not profit. There is no payment due for his rescue of the Red Cattle, 'imprisoned' on an island under the control of the three-bodied Geryon, his double-headed dog, and a mysterious shepherd who has looked after the red cattle for time immemorial. I knew that much, but what to make of the clues John had left me?

I was no wiser when the train arrived at Euston some two hours later – My legal team knew not to expect me before midday on a Monday; I put in the extra hours during the week, no-one doubted that. I had a short time to make some sense of it all. Within minutes, I was speeding in a red underground train beneath the streets of the City and towards Monument – the tube station with the same name as the tower on the mysterious picture. Minutes later, I emerged into the unexpectedly bright sunshine and looked up at my destination. The tower, arrowing into the clear sky, had been built in the seventeenth century to commemorate the Great Fire of London, and was designed by Christopher Wren. It is capped by a blazing gold sculpture symbolising the Great Fire, itself.

There are three hundred and eleven steps to get to the golden viewing platform which forms the base of the massive sculpture. I am a fit person, but each circuit of that spiral was increasingly painful – in heels. On the third, I stopped, mouth open. A larger scale red paper man was fastened to the wall of the ascending stairwell. There was no other sign. I stopped and stared at it, happy to have any excuse to rest my feet and get my breath back. He had been here–and obviously just ahead of me…

After three further circuits of the spiral, I encountered another paper man on the stairway wall; but this one was black. Again, there was no other reference to my increasingly lonely quest.

The final figure came, as expected, on the ninth circuit, but this time the paper man was white. Red, black, white. The sequence triggered a distant memory of a conversation John and I had about the time we were beginning to talk about the esoteric. Now, I remembered that he had said that, from an ancient British perspective, the generic colours of the Goddess were red, black and white... Was I ascending, with much effort, through these colours? Would John be waiting for me at the top?

My heart was hammering in my chest, but I pushed on, clicking in a much slower rhythm on the old stone spiral. With my head hanging on my gasping chest, I staggered onto the viewing platform and looked, anxiously, around. I had to suppress a small sob when I found I was alone. The golden light, reflected from the massive, burning sculpture above me, was intense...but, slumped against the safety rail and gazing down the sixty metre drop to see the masses of people below, I knew nothing...

The revelations started when I began to descend. Passing the white paper man, I suddenly realised that the two-headed dog was a reference to the above and the below, and that Herakles had moved – had graduated – in the certainty of his own light to a being whose home was the above, the causal layer of all Being. He had therefore 'slain' the lower, seeing it for the resultant, if useful, shadow it was.

When I reached the black paper man, I became aware that the Shepherd in the story – the one guarding the red cattle – had been spared by the hero because he represented the one who looked after the cattle; in human terms, the mind of man, woven, in a seemingly inextricable pattern, into the fibres of his being. Of course he had been spared – he was the way forward, once unity of being was established.

Crossing the final threshold of the red paper man, I realised with a smile that I was about to re-enter the world of the red cattle, that the three bodies represented our old friends the instinctive man, the emotional man and the intellectual man – all at odds with each other until the single arrow of redemptive purpose bore through them, as Heracles' fiery arrow had finally done, not killing them, but fusing them all into a single entity, capable of being guided from above...

And now I had travelled up and then down that arrow, uniting the totality of my experience with John.

The golden sunlight streamed through the portal of the entrance. But, to my right something else red caught my eye. A scarlet rose had been taped to the old, rusty metal of exit's door frame. With tears forming in my eyes, I took it...knowing it was for me.

And then I was in the street, and people were staring at me. Everywhere I turned people were curious about the woman with the flower in her hands, walking into a new world seen for the first time.

I wanted to give the rose to them, but I had only one rose and there were so many of them. How could I do that?

The sun shone at my back, I could feel its warmth on my head. I did not know what to do, but the previous sense of panic and confusion belonged to another world. In this one, the need to do something would be accompanied by the knowledge of what to do. That, I knew with a certainty.

Somewhere nearby, John might be watching... But it no longer mattered. Everything that mattered was here... Everything that mattered was now...

About the Author

Steve Tanham is the Founding Director of the Silent Eye School of Consciousness. The School seeks to provide a new approach to an ancient vision, a way of working that dovetails with everyday life in our busy world and builds a Temple of the Moment in the consciousness of the student. Steve maintains a personal blog, Sun in Gemini, which can be found at https://stevetanham.wordpress.com/.

Steve is also the author of The Beast in the Café, which tells the journey of an ordinary man... a writer...whose world is turned upside down by an insistent Pomeranian and his mysterious owner. Everyday objects become the tools that lead first to knowledge, then to the glimmering of understanding...

The Silent Eye School of Consciousness is a modern Mystery School that seeks to allow its students to find the inherent magic in living and being. With students around the world the School offers a fully supervised and practical correspondence course that explores the self through guided inner journeys and daily exercises. It also offers workshops that combine sacred drama, lectures and informal gatherings in the landscape that bring the teachings to life in a vivid and exciting format. The Silent Eye operates on a not-for profit basis. Full details of the School may be found on the official website: www.thesilenteye.co.uk

The Silent Eye
a modern mystery school